Toe Tagz 2

D1452497

Ah'Million

**Lock Down Publications and Ca$h
Presents**

Toe Tagz 2

A Novel by *Ah'Million*

Ah'Million

Lock Down Publications
P.O. Box 870494
Mesquite, Tx 75187

Visit our website @
www.lockdownpublications.com

Lock Down Publications
Like our page on Facebook: Lock Down Publications @
www.facebook.com/lockdownpublications.ldp
Cover design and layout by: **Dynasty Cover Me**
Book interior design by: **Shawn Walker**
Edited by: **Sunny Giovanni**

Stay Connected with Us!

Text **LOCKDOWN** to 22828 to stay up-to-date with new releases, sneak peaks, contests and more…

Thank you.

Submission Guideline.

Submit the first three chapters of your completed manuscript to ldpsubmissions@gmail.com, subject line: Your book's title. The manuscript must be in a .doc file and sent as an attachment. Document should be in Times New Roman, double spaced and in size 12 font. Also, provide your synopsis and full contact information. If sending multiple submissions, they must each be in a separate email.

Have a story but no way to send it electronically? You can still submit to LDP/Ca$h Presents. Send in the first three chapters, written or typed, of your completed manuscript to:

LDP: Submissions Dept
Po Box 870494
Mesquite, Tx 75187

DO NOT send original manuscript. Must be a duplicate.

Provide your synopsis and a cover letter containing your full contact information.

Thanks for considering LDP and Ca$h Presents.

ACKNOWLEDGMENTS

I want to thank God, first and foremost, for blessing me with this undeniable talent. I want to thank my mother, Suga Momma, my brothers—Donkey and Munsta. Shout out to Chocolate Drop, and my friend Jasper who was a huge help. Bryeshia, I love you. None of this has been easy. This journey almost over, but never this pen and pad. Also, I want to thank all of those on lock who supported the movement. I love those who love me. And for those who don't, oh well. Unc, Pops! I love ya. Enjoy.

P.S. This for my brothers. Free Donkey and Munsta.

Ah'Million

INTRO
PREVIOUSLY...

"Baby, are you okay?" Bre yelled from the other side of the door.

"Yeah, I'm good." Mun mumbled as loud as he could, as beads of sweat formed in his forehead.

Low groans escaped Mun's mouth as he strained to release his vowels. The food that they'd eaten earlier had upset his stomach.

Five-star restaurant my ass! He fumed.

The sound of his phone ringing startled him. He knew from the ringtone that it was Donk, so he grabbed the phone of off the sink counter.

"Yeah?"

"You good?" Donk asked.

"Yeah, I'm good."

"Bruh, is Bre around you?"

"Nah. Why? What's up?" Mun was confused by Donk's tone.

"Look fam, you better watch that bitch. She's the one that set me up the day I got shot. I have solid evidence," Donk replied with certainty.

"Whaaatttt?" Mun was stunned.

"Yeah bruh. Facts!" said Donk.

"Say no more."

Mun hung up the phone and swallowed the lump in his throat. He hadn't known Bre was to be the grimy type, but she had held back things from him. The shit with Danielle, mainly. And when Mun reevaluated some things, he recalled catching her starring hard at Donk from time to time. He hadn't called her out on it because her eyes were the doors to her soul, and Mun considered it a blessing to be able to read a person's soul.

He wiped his ass and washed his hands. After thinking about going to get his gun from under his pillow, Mun decided to just play things cool. When he opened the bathroom door, Bre was sitting on the edge of the bed watching television. As soon as he stepped out, Bre brought Mun's .44 Magnum from underneath her shirt and stood to her feet.

With the gun aimed directly at Mun, she spoke slowly. "First it was the hustle, then it was Quaylo, and now it's Donk. I gave you all of me, but I was always second on your life. I--"

"Really?" Mun yelled, cutting her off. "Those are my loved ones. My family!"

A knock on the door drew their attention. Bre kept the gun on Mun while she moved to the door and looked through the peep-hole.

Boom!

A shotgun blast blew through the door and splattered Bre's brains all over the ceiling. Mun thought Donk had saved him again until the door swung in and he saw Donatello's face. Mun's heart rate exploded. He was now staring down the barrel of a sawed-off.

"You thought you are going to live freely after taking the life of my beloved niece?" Donatello growled. "Surely, you didn't think I would allow that."

Donatello inched closer and pressed the barrel of the shotgun to the tip of Mon's nose.

"Look, Donatello--"

"Shut the fuck up! You took her life and now I'm going to take yours...."

PROLOGUE
7 years later

"PJ!" Kadejah yelled jumping out of the bed and flicking on the light switch.

"Huh?" PJ groaned softly, adjusting the covers over his head to keep the light from seeping in.

Kadejah and PJ had their own room but PJ's fear of the darkness led him to Kadejah's room every night. She awoke each morning to find PJ asleep beside her bed on the floor. "Come on, PJ, we got to get ready for school!" Kadejah shouted while retrieving her clothes from her closet, alarmed at the fact she actually had fallen asleep to be awakened by the alarm on her nightstand. Kadejah was so anxious to attend school the next morning. She found herself lying in bed staring at the walls in the wee hours of the night, bored. She tried different styles with her box braids until she discovered the right one. She even went as far as putting on the uniform she would wear; the shoes and Chanel satchel while doing a full 360 in the full-length mirror.

With everything that had taken place in the area where Donk grew up, he finally decided to leave everything behind and move out further in a more suburban area. However, he understood the adversity of changing schools, so he allowed PJ and Kadejah to attend the same school.

PJ finally forced himself off the floor before grabbing his blanket, tucking it underneath his arm and heading to his room.

Singing along to Cardi B's Bodak *Yellow* while ironing her white Hollister uniform shirt, Kadejah nearly burned herself when she noticed the shadow out her peripheral. "Uncle Donk! You scared me." She gasped before placing her hand on her chest.

"Oh, you don't have to dance, you make money moves? Huh?" He quoted Cardi B's lyrics. "So, what you have on the rent?" Donk asked Kadejah playfully. At the age of thirteen Kadejah had blossomed into a beautiful young lady. She was the spitting image of her mother Quaylo; it was unreal.

11

"Come on, Uncle Donk, you know all my funds come from you," she admitted while grinning as she unplugged the iron.

"Well, while you jamming, put a little pep in your step so we can go ahead and enroll y'all," Donk stated before turning on his heels.

PJ was eleven years old and attending elementary school; it was his last year. However, it was Kadejah's first year of middle school. Donk walked in on PJ who was brushing his hair in the full-length mirror. His clothes were starched to perfection, and his cologne lingered; it wasn't loud and cheap, but exquisite and smooth. Donk had taken PJ into his home when he was just 3 years old, along with his mother Persuasia. Despite Donk losing all the family he had, he'd finally come to the realization that death is inevitable and we're all alone to face it. No amount of cash or protection can prevent it.

He lost his sister Quaylo first, to only find out it was a friend of the fam that caused her demise. Then, his mother Rochelle to a deadly disease, and last his brother Mun who lost his life to a bitch that took her own as well. Luckily, through all the pain, he managed to obtain Kadejah and vowed to protect her with everything in him.

"Aye, fly guy! You ready?" Donk called out as he leaned his tall frame against the entry, smiling at PJ. Donk taught PJ a lot of things, but PJ was very observant as well. It was things he picked up on, just by watching Donk. He admired everything about Donk. That's why Donk was very cautious of the things he did and said around him. He even made Kadejah promise to keep the things she witnessed to herself. Donk didn't mind giving the game to Kadejah raw and uncut, exposing the real, since she'd been exposed to so much at a young age.

Kadejah knew there was more to life than video games, cartoons and Barbie dolls. Her once gullible eyes had witnessed violence, drama, incarceration and death firsthand. She knew there was an effect to every cause and a consequence for every action whether it was good or bad. He hated the fact she experienced as much in her short life span. If only Quaylo hadn't given her up for adoption at birth, the less she would've encountered.

"I'm ready." PJ announced with his yellow, black, and turquoise off-white sneakers in his hand.

"Okay, let me go throw on some clothes and we'll meet y'all in the front room," Donk shot back before stepping into the hallway. The closer he got to his bedroom, the sweet scent lingered down the hallway. He had awakened Persuasia minutes before going to check on the kids. He knew she needed a head start to get dressed. He never understood why it took women so long to get themselves together. He quietly entered the room, closing the door behind him, immediately spotting Persuasia getting dressed inside the bathroom. Her hair was pinned up as she pulled the small white Versace blouse over her head. "Um-mm." Donk cleared his throat.

"You not slick. I heard you when you come in," she stated never looking up from the mirror.

"I just knew you was going to still be running around half naked." Donk replied walking past her to retrieve his clothes, slapping her on the ass as he bypassed.

Donk and Persuaia were a true example of a power couple. Together or apart they received lots of attention. She was banging and he was dripping. She was bossy and strong-minded; Donk was domineering and imperial. Automatically assuming they possessed aloof personalities due to they're swagger, they were actually very down to earth.

Persuasia stood in the bathroom mirror adjusting her clothes and checking out her make-up. Little did Donk know she has eyeing him out the corner of her eye while he got dressed. She admired him and was deeply attracted to Donk. Things as petty as pulling up his pants she found fascinating. His swag, his confidence, demeanor and everything else was attractive. "Okay, I'm ready, bae," Persuasia announced walking out of the bathroom; hair up. Her coal black, curly hair fell past her shoulders and hung freely, and her pink lips made her look exotic. She was rocking a white Versace blouse, a tight pair of J Brand jeans, white and

13

beige Jimmy Choo pumps and an almond brown Hermes bag. Donk stood to his feet and scanned the nicely decorated bedroom before retrieving his car keys from the nightstand.

Nothing went unnoticed with Donk; he was very attentive and calculated. The house reeked of Clorox and Pine Sol, the AC stayed on high which often made the house smell and feel like a hospital. Persuasia pranced up ahead while Donk surveyed each room. Kadejah's room was clearly empty, yet he could still hear Cardi B coming from the speaker. He walked in and turned off the iPod. Taking one last look around the room, he left and made his way across the hall to PJs. The scent of his cologne still lingered around the room, but it was incredulously organized. Nothing whatsoever out of place, this brought a smile to Donk's face. Although PJ was eleven years old, he acted a lot older. Like my grandma would say, "That boy been here before."

The familiar scent resurfaced old memories and immediately he thought of Mun. Tears begin to well in Donk's eyes, but weeping, grief, sorrow, and anything else of that sort no longer lived in him. The last time Donk shed tears was a few years ago when he came to the realization Mun had left, never to return, and he'll never see him again. To Donk's knowledge Mun had went on vacation to Jamaica with Bre, whom he had been with three years. He was given some valuable information regarding Bre's disloyalty, so Donk contacted Mun while he was out there, revealing that Bre was a fraud, counterfeit as a three dollar bill, and to watch out. That was the last time Donk spoke to Mun. Here it was seven years later, still no sign of Mun.

Many nights, Donk cried until he drifted off to sleep, awakening the next morning thinking the night before was all a dream until he looked into the mirror, immediately spotting his swollen eyes. You would've thought he had an allergic reaction as he continued to peer through the glass at his reflection that resembled a raccoon by the eyes. The agony was evident.

"Y'all ready?" Donk asked entering the living room, where everyone awaited. In response they all stood to their feet and made their exit. Donk surveyed the house one last time before closing the door behind him.

Over the past few years so much had changed. Nothing of detriment but more acceptance and adaptation after losing the ones who loved him unconditionally and knew him best. Today he can finally say he's okay. Don't misconstrue it, he's going to mourn them until he joins them but he's no longer angry at society or upset with himself. He gave his burdens to the almighty while taking care of the family he has now.

Persuasia loved every moment spent with her new family. Donk treated her like a queen and her son like a prince. He was a different caliber and she had the upmost respect for him. He was a real nigga before anything else; getting money came second. Persuasia listened to PJ and Kadejah sing along to the music. Their voices became faint as she drifted off to the day she met Donk. She was so caught up in her thoughts she didn't feel the tap on her shoulder. She jumped, caught off guard.

PJ immediately laughed at her reaction. "Momma, I want to go to school with Kadejah," PJ spoke a little above a whisper.

She slightly turned to face him, admiring his growth. "You can't, baby. Kadejah is older than you. Next year you'll be able to go."

"Alright," PJ responded a bit agitated, leaning back in his seat.

Persuasia continued to gaze out the window reflecting on her life before meeting Donk. The beautiful five-bedroom, four bathroom and six car garage home caught her eye the first day she laid eyes on it. She knew it was difficult for Donk to sell his mother's house, but it held way too many memories that Donk attempted to but could not withstand.

Ah'Million

CHAPTER 1
DONK

Me and Persuasia figured enrolling PJ and Kadejah wouldn't be a problem. We figured since PJ was the youngest they'd enroll him first. Upon entering W.T. Brown elementary school we were greeted by a heavy-set Hispanic lady.

"Right this way," she mumbled as if she had been at work for hours already when really her day just started close to an hour ago.

We rounded the corner in route to the principal's office. PJ dragged behind not feeling the idea of attending school without Kadejah. Despite the fact Kadejah was capable of taking care of herself, PJ made a vow to me that he would protect his sister and he despised the idea of letting me down.

"How are you all today?" The male principal asked, flashing his pearly whites. The tall black man looked to be in his mid-forties. He was dressed in a cheap navy-blue suit and a shiny pair of black Stacy Adams that looked as if he shined them one too many times. His hair was cut to perfection. As a matter of fact, his edge up resembled the comedian Steve Harvey's.

"Were doing fine." Persuasia responded politely.

"Are they both attending W.T. Brown?" He asked.

"No, just Prichard. He's going to the sixth grade." Persuasia stated, pointing at an uninterested PJ.

"Do you stay in the area, Mrs. And Mr…" He paused awaiting an answer.

"Richards!" I spoke up, firmly shaking the principal's hand.

"I'm Mr. Frazier. I asked because June 16th we sent out the notices informing the parents that the sixth-grade students will be moved to the junior high school which will consist of sixth, seventh and eighth grade students."

I looked back at a grinning PJ. This was right up his alley.

"Thank you, Mr. Frazier, have a good day," Persuasia stated before turning on her heels while the rest of us followed suit.

Enrolling Kadejah and PJ wasn't a problem. Once the counselor handed them their schedules, PJ and Kadejah headed down the empty hall.

"Call me when y'all ready," I called out before they disappeared around the corner.

"Okay!" they shouted in unison. PJ bent down to tuck his pants behind the tongue of his shoe, immediately reaching into his back pocket retrieving the crisp white towel and removing the blemish.

"He gon' be just like me," I whispered to Persuasia while standing at the opposite end of the hallway with both hands tucked inside my pockets.

"She is too," Persuasia shot back, staring in Kadejah's direction.

Kadejah wore an all-white Gucci polo shirt and navy-blue Hollister joggers with a pair of Gucci sneakers and a Gucci *Dive* bracelet watch. Her navy blue and white Nike fanny pack rested around her waist as she bent down to tease her shoestrings. They both turned around and waved goodbye before disappearing around the corner.

I sat behind the wheel of my black Cadillac Escalade while I bobbed my head to Yella Beezy's latest hit *That's on Me Baby*. I kept my eyes trained on the streets, being extra cautious of my surroundings. I glanced down at my Rolex then immediately noticed Pedro hopping out of his burgundy Denali truck.

Pedro walked over and opened the passenger side of my truck, tossing the black duffel bag inside before climbing in. "It's all there," he assured.

I reached around and grabbed the shopping bag that was on the floor in the backseat. We exchanged bags and quickly inspected the contents inside. Pedro had been my connect for years. I met him a year after Mun passed.

"Same time and location next week, my friend," Pedro stated exiting the truck.

"Nice doing business with you." I smiled before pulling off. Life was good and business was even better. I just wish Quaylo and Mun were here to share the wealth.

Ah'Million

CHAPTER 2
LIL' TIM

I stood in the breezeway of my four-bedroom home smoking a blunt and scrolling down the newsfeed on my Facebook when the loud music coming in my direction broke my concentration. Seeing that it was Donk, a smile slowly spread across my face. I was always ecstatic to see my dawg. Donk was the one who offered me the second in command position at sixteen when Mun got knocked and Rico committed suicide.

Donk hopped out the truck looking like a check. His yellow gold chain hung low on top of his crispy white Prada V-neck. His navy-blue Hanes brief boxers were slightly exposed as he tugged on his black and gold Gucci belt that was looped perfectly through his light denim Levi shorts. Donk was as hood and as masculine as they came but you couldn't help but notice his freshly pedicured toes that were exposed in his Bally flip flops.

"What's up, boy!" He greeted joyfully.

"Chilling on it, fam," I responded, pulling Donk in for a quick embrace.

"What time you heading out?" Donk asked.

"In about an hour. Bando at the car wash in the West. Lil' Reggie at the spot. I'm gon' go ahead and pull up on both of them niggas to collect, and make sure everything is everything. Feel me?" I spoke in between puffs. I extended my arm toward Donk in an attempt to pass him the Spliff.

"Nah, nigga, I'm good. I ain't fucking with that loud no more. I don't want that shit around them youngins. They don't need to be picking up no bad habits," Donk stated; slowly gazing over the quiet neighborhood.

"Yeah, you right. Man, you love them kids. I wish I could just quit cold turkey," I retorted.

"Come on, let's go ahead and break this shit down. I got to meet up with this dude in the Nawf to go check out this building for this sports bar," Donk stated retrieving the duffel bag from his truck.

"Hell yeah. I almost forgot! I'm gon' try and meet you up there. If it's a go, you gon' start putting shit in motion today, right?" I asked, ecstatic.

"You already know!"

***

"Aye! Bando leave that thot where she at. I need to holler at you!" I yelled over the loud music coming from the car speaker. Today was like any other day in the hood. The carwash on Bruton was full of fiends, thot's and hood niggas as usual. Peach hit me off with a little sloppy toppy and eggs in bed before I left her crib this morning.

"What's up, boy?" Bando asked, dapping me up. Bando was just nineteen years old, a born hustler with a mentality of an old head.

I met Bando two years ago. I was at a party in Atlanta, somewhere I had no business being. I couldn't refrain from going. Everybody that was somebody was there, and I was posted up like a light post, looking for a chocolate drop. I wasn't in the club five minutes before the thots start flocking. Club Elite was supposedly a new club, and tonight was the Grand Opening. The set up was nice if you ask me. Classy and elegant with expensive taste, it was ratchets shaking ass, but the place wasn't ratchet at all. I swaggered to the bar, catching glances in different directions. The Cartier glasses that covered my eyes only enhanced my fit. I was sporting a red, black, and gold Gucci track suit.

"Aye, let me get two shots of Henney," I requested, placing the twenty dollar bill on the counter.

"You can have whatever you like," the Puerto Rican bartender stated. She had deep dimples like Lauren London and a nice set of teeth. Her hair was jet black and full of curls, but it was obviously a weave. She had an accent that immediately grasped my attention.

"Oh, is that right?" I shot back flirtatiously.

"Hold on, don't go nowhere," she snapped, rushing over to the line of customers that repeatedly used their hands to get her attention.

I carefully watched shorty do her thing with the other customers. She must've been really digging my swag 'cause through all the commotion she kept looking back at me. The loud commotion behind me caught my attention instantly. Dude was about 6'4" with little weight on him, and I assumed shorty he was roughing up was his. I watched in disdain at the absurd sight. I just never understood dudes that beat women. Before I beat a bitch, I'm gone leave that bitch. I refuse to degrade what I stand for and go against my morals and beliefs. Nope. Right idea. Wrong dude. Shorty was cute but ratchet. She hollered effortlessly while dude dragged her by her bra strap through the club. I tried to make out what he was saying but it was difficult due to the loud music.

"Hey, can I get some attention now?" The amiable bartender asked as she sat her hand on top of mine.

"I got a little time to kick it, what's up?"

Meanwhile in the dressing room

"Dino, stop, please. I'm sorry!" Honey yelled out breathlessly.

Dino continued to punch her in the face. Her eye immediately closed after the first strike. Blood oozed from her lip and nose as she continued to kick her feet in an attempt to get free. "I'll stop when I feel like it. I bet you won't play with my money next time," Dino stated with no signs of fatigue.

The dressing room was surprisingly empty on this particular night. Money was all over the place and none of the ladies wanted to miss out. Hence, Honey lost all strength and her legs gave out, making a loud thud once her six-inch pumps connected with the tile floor.

"Bitch," Dino cursed, kicking her in the abs, causing Honey to curl into a fetal position. He spat in her face then proceeded out of the dressing room.

***

"So, since it'll be closing time in an hour, can we take this back to your place?" The bartender suggested, tracing her lips with her tongue.

"Ma, what's your name?" I asked sarcastically.

With a hint of embarrassment, she quickly said. "Stacy. Um, it's Stacy. Stacy Tokes."

"Oh, okay, but you could've kept the last name. I'm not trying to run a background check," I joked.

"So, you c—"

I stopped her in midsentence when ol' boy who I saw beating the stripper chick appeared behind me.

"Stacy, what's up?" He asked in a threatening tone, looking back and forth between me and her. My face instantly twisted into a menacing scowl.

"What? Dino, let me do me," she retorted.

"I'm saying, y'all been chopping it up for some time now. Bitch, time is money." Dino stated, sizing me up.

"Say, look out. This yo bitch?" I asked standing to my feet. My mug never left 'cause I wanted this cat to know ain't no pressure on no smoke. If you act like you want it, I'm on yo' ass.

"This my hoe, and I'm hoe-checking. If you ain't talking 'bout spending no money, go 'bout your business." Dino spoke in a calm yet serious tone. His eyes were sharp like daggers but I wasn't bothered by none of that shit.

"Nigga, look at me. I ain't never paid for no pussy. The way she holding a nigga up, she act like she want to pay me!" I stated before downing my shot of Hennessey. Dino had fire in his eyes. I inched closer. "Do me like you just did that hoe and get ya issue," I spat through clenched teeth. I removed my shades and placed them in my pocket, thinking Dino would pop off.

Instead, he whistled for back up, and before I knew it I was surrounded. Seventeen shots was all I had, and from the looks of it I was outnumbered. The smirk on Dino's face made me feel some type of way, but I didn't show it. I wasn't going to go out without a fight.

"Aye, Dino! Pookie say you and your peeps got to go. It's some major cats here tonight and he can't have your people tearing up the place." The bouncer firmly stated.

"This ain't over, nigga!" One of the dudes with Dino yelled. He was a yes man. His comment didn't move me at all, but I was relieved, 'cause it gave me a better chance at a fair fight.

Dino winked and turned away, but I could tell from the look he gave me it was far from over.

Once they were all gone, I placed my shades on my eyes and went to enjoy myself.

"Look, I'm so—"

I quickly raised my hand, cutting Stacy short. "Save that. You good," I stated and proceeded on. I made my way through the packed club at a slow pace. Niggas was dancing harder than the females.

"Aye! Lil' Tim! What's good, baby?"

I squinted my eyes to make out the familiar face. "Chris! Damn! Where you been at?" I yelled, shocked to see Chris after believing all the death rumors.

"Man, I had to move around; wasn't shit in Dallas," Chris responded convincingly.

"Yeah, you ain't never lied," I shot back.

"You good? Ain't shit changed. You still my li'l homie!" Chris asked full of concern. Chris was quite older than me. He stood six feet even, about two hundred and fifty pounds. He kind of put you in the mind of Rick Ross. He rocked a bald fade with the Tyson part. His goatee wasn't thick; it was a more like a peach fuzz, but it was neatly lined up on every side as if he went to the barber shop twice a week.

As a youngin' Chris would give me school money or buy me a pair of shoes here and there, but he would never put me in the game 'cause he didn't want to be the reason something happen to me, living that lifestyle. To him my age had a lot to do with it. That's why I loved Donk and Mun the way I did, 'cause they believed in me and gave me a chance when no one else would take me seriously.

"Yeah, Chris, I'm straight. Life can't get no better, man. Let me get your number doe'. I want to catch up and show you how I'm living." I stated, removing my Samsung Galaxy from my pocket. I sat next to one of the chicks who was seated on the plush sectional.

The chick that sat beside Chris was gorgeous, but she put me in the mind of the chick that played Cleo's girlfriend on the movie *Set it Off*. She just sat there smiling and shit but never uttered a word. Her skin was the color of a Starbuck's Frappe. Her hair was short like Amber Rose with a burgundy-reddish tint. Her eyebrows were thick and neatly arched. They also matched her hair color. She had a beautiful set of teeth and a bottom lip piercing on the left side that complimented her smile. Even though she was seated I could tell she had a banging body in the multi colored Versace body suit she sported.

"Aye, y'all give me and my boy some privacy." Chris demanded, slapping the chick in the Versace suit on the ass. "That's Stasha." He stated, catching my drift of curiosity.

"Stasha? Okay," I repeated, nodding my head in approval as I surveyed the club.

"Yeah, Stasha my bottom bitch. I got out the drug game and started investing my time and everything else into these hoes," Chris said with a serious look in his eyes.

"As a matter of fact, I do got one problem," I quickly spoke up, almost forgetting the beef with Dino.

"What's up?" He asked scooting to the edge of his seat.

"I just got into it with some simp ass nigga name Dino, and I got a feeling him and his chick going to be waiting outside the club for me." I admitted.

"Dino?" He repeated as if the name was unfamiliar, however his eyes said different.

"Yeah, tall dude." I described.

"Oh yeah. I know that foo. He's exactly what you called him; a ol' simp ass nigga. I done had a few run-ins with dude but he always come correct so I let him make it. But if nigga want beef, one call and we'll shut this bitch down," Chris argued, standing to his feet.

"Nah, big homie, I'm not trying to fuck the city up. I just need you to make sure them niggas don't try to jump me or air my shit out."

"Oh, that's overstood. Let's go. Stasha, round up! It's time to go!" Chris yelled at Stasha who was standing a few feet away talking to a guy at the bar. Let me specify that; she was rubbing on the guy's head while he was doing all the talking. Once she heard Chris's voice, she quickly dismissed the funny looking but expensively dressed dude and went searching for the other girls.

"Nah, I'm not gon' let that fuck boy fuck up my night. I'm trying to kick it until they shut this bitch down for the night." I stated peering up at him from my seat.

Chris looked at me with uncertainty in his eyes as he began to scratch his head. He reached for his goatee and lightly stroked his facial hair before sitting down. "We gon' chill, yougin, but soon they announce last call for alcohol, I'm on that nigga ass." Chris expressed, picking up his drink.

Me and Chris talked for what felt like hours, the ladies joined us in between time, and I was formally introduced to Stasha. She wasn't a mute, but she wasn't talkative either, and that was fine with me. I let Millie, Sydney, and Ah'rya entertain me for the night. These ladies weren't ratchet, busted up chicks, they were top notch. Ah'rya hit me with some lip service I'll never forget, but my feelings don't go through the veins in my dick. I can dib then scram like it ain't shit. That's why I had no problem letting Millie give me some neck next. Sydney wanted a piece of the pie too, but I wasn't gone continue to let these bitches drain me dry and it was a possibility my life was in danger.

A few laughs and drinks later the DJ announced the last song for the night. *I Know* by Yo Gotti and Rich Homie Quan blasted through the speakers and I instantly rose to my feet, rapping along to the lyrics. Full of liquor I began to smoothly ride the beat, and before I knew it I was swaying, holding my nuts. Only real niggas could relate, and I felt like they couldn't have ended the night with a better song.

"Pocket full of money, boy, I know the feeling!" I quoted winding down.

"You staying the night in the A? Or you heading back to the D?" Chris asked standing to his feet.

"I got some shit to handle, fam. I'm gon' go ahead and push back to my city."

"It can't wait until tomorrow? What's the rush?" He asked curiously.

"Nah, big homie, it can't," I responded, avoiding his question.

"Alright. Come on. Let's get out of here. Make sure Dino ain't trying no sneak shit."

"Daddy, Honey was found unconscious in the dressing room. Ah'rya helping her pull herself together now," Sasha stated in a low tone.

"Alright," Chris responded, quickly dismissing Stasha as he walked away in the opposite direction toward the exit. Damn, this nigga had all type of hoes.

Who the hell is Honey? I thought while following Chris out of the club. The DJ was in the middle of his last announcement. Shorties were telling their homegirl's bye and were leaving with the nigga they exchanged glances with all night. I made eye contact with Stacy while she was wiping down the bar, but I turned my head in a different direction, even though she couldn't see my eyes behind the expensive shades.

The cool breeze hit me like a ton of bricks as soon as I stepped out the club.

"Aye, me and my gals might swing through tomorrow. I'll let you know though. Stasha might have something else planned." Chris told the guy who stood outside in front of the club. He wore a cream-colored Burberry suit with the matching loafers. I assume he was the owner. He put me in the mind of a light skinned Kevin Hart.

"Yeah, do that so I can have your section reserved." He responded, tossing the cigar to the ground mashing it with his foot. "Another protégé?" He looked at Chris curiously.

"Nah, this my little homie from around the way. Been a minute since I saw him. We were just catching up." Chris sated. "Lil' Tim, this Murdock. Murdock, this Lil' Tim." We acknowledged one another with a nod.

"Alright, big homie. The coast looks pretty clear. I'm gon' go ahead and shoot back to my city," I spoke while pounding fists with Chris.

"I told you that nigga wasn't about shit. Which way you heading? I'm going to follow you to the city limit." Chris suggested.

"I'm going to stop at the Exxon first, but it's no need for you to follow me. I'm good from here," I assured slowly backpedaling to my whip.

With a simple nod Chris stood motionless in front of the club until I was inside my money green Jeep SRT. I turned up the volume as Kevin Gates blasted through the speakers. I swerved out the lot and headed in the direction of the Exxon, which only took five minutes to reach. I killed the engine and climbed out. A thin, poorly dressed Arabian guy stood behind the counter. It looked like he'd just opened his eyes when the doorbell sounded.

"Give me fifty on pump two," I said, handing him a fifty-dollar bill.

As soon as I opened the door to exit the store, I felt a hard object connect with my mouth. It had to be a gun, metal bat, or brass knuckles; either one. Immediately after the blow I fell to one knee. I tried regaining my composure but the impact of the second hit that connected with my jaw caused me to lose balance and drop to both knees. I yelped out in pain as the attacker kicked me in my stomach. Then, I fell face-first onto the pavement.

I could feel the warm blood trickling down my face as I thought about Chris ass. Always trying to stand on my own, right then and there, I regretted the fact I didn't tell him to follow me. It's cool, dude caught me slipping. I tried to block my face with my arms, but it was useless. Several punches from several niggas slipped through the barrier I tried to maintain, yet several connected. My ribs were on fire and all I could do was clinch every muscle in my body from my jaw to my ass cheeks just so the pain would subside and I could endure the next punch.

***

Bando sat in his all black Crown Victoria looking for the perfect opportunity to run up in the gas station, when he saw an all-black Denali truck park on the side of the store. *Hell nah, these niggas 'bout to take my lick*, he thought, sitting up straight in his seat as soon as he exited the store. A gang of men went to work on him. The sight in front of Bando was horrendous. Nonetheless he tried to focus on his own mission, but the horrible sight wouldn't allow him to focus on the task at hand.

Fuck this, he said to himself before hopping out of his whip. He pulled up his jeans by the crotch and quickly strolled toward the action. As he grew closer he slowed his pace toward the action, quickly scanning his surroundings. Bando puffed on the blunt that dangled from his lips. With slooped feet he inched closer and pulled the trigger on his .40 Glock. *Bock! Bock! Bock! Bock! Bock!* Bando let his .40 spit, aiming to hit all eight men.

"What the fuck! Let's get out of here; they shooting!" The men yelled, trying to scramble free. Three of the men died instantly. Two used they're forearms to crawl away from the mayhem, and the rest flopped like fish to avoid a bullet wound, while Bando walked up on severely beaten Lil' Tim.

Hearing dude's voice was like ice water to a nigga in hell. I effortlessly dropped my arms that I uselessly attempted to protect my face. I knew I was banged up pretty bad. When I made eye contact with the guy that stood over me, I honestly thought Chris was somewhere nearby and he sent one of his goons to help me, but I was wrong. I tried opening my mouth to speak but a sharp pain hit me, abruptly traveling from my spine and up to my neck. "Fuck!" I howled in pain.

"Come on." He helped me to my feet then guided me to his car. I staggered but I finally made it as he opened the passenger door. "I'll be right back. I got to snatch the tapes," he stated, tossing the blunt to the ground before making a dash inside the store. He was back in less than five minutes, seated in the driver's seat.

"I'm Lil' Tim." I struggled, gripping my oblique.

"Bando. Buckle up," he responded as he sped off. Since that night, me and Bando had been locked in. He came to visit me in my city and never went back to his. Chris eventually came back to Dallas once and for all.

"How shit looking so far?" I asked, posted up on the hood of my candy red Cadillac STS.

"I got a couple OZ's left. I was just about to hit you up." He responded with his eyes glued to the hood rat's ass that bypassed us. Bando was mature in a lot of ways, but when it came to pussy he was as frail as a 90-year-old man.

"Okay, bet. Follow me to the spot. I'm gon' hit you off then I'll link up with you later. Me and Donk heading to the Nawf to check out this spot for his sports bar."

Ah'Million

CHAPTER 3
KADEJAH

"Hey, Kadejah!" old peers shouted once we bypassed one another. I was so ready for this school year to be over with so I could advance to high school.

"Aye, sis, what lunch you got?" PJ asked while we strolled down the long hallway.

"Um…let me see." I replied, retrieving the schedule from my purse. "Uh, excuse me." I continued, accidentally bumping into a light skinned, big boned chick with acne all over her face.

"Yeah, excuse you," she shot back with attitude.

"Hold on. Watch out, PJ," I stated, walking in front of him. "You want smoke?" I asked with a mug on my face, already in the process of removing my jewelry and handbag.

Without responding she began to backpedal, bumping into other people, trying to get out of sight.

"Her ol' raggedy ass got the nerve to talk shit and she rocking wookies." I commented loudly, a bit upset. Wookies was another word for *knock-off*.

"Ha! Ha! Ha! Girl, come on. I don't even know why these people would try and gas you up." PJ commented, lightly shoving me in my lower back.

"Anyways, I got C lunch. Which one do you have?"

"I got B," PJ confirmed, leaning up against the locker with one leg off the ground.

"I'll just—" Before I could respond, a familiar face came into view, diverting my attention.

"Hey, Kadejah." The girl smiled coyly looking toward the ground.

"Arianna? Oh my God!"

Arianna slowly looked up sheepishly matching my gaze.

Despite the bedroom eyes, I reached out and wrapped my arms tightly around her tiny frame. I couldn't believe it was her in the flesh after all these years. Discreetly peering at her wardrobe I instantly felt sorry for Arianna. Recanting my less fortunate days before I ran into the arms of Bre, Uncle Mun and Donk.

Ring! Ring! Disregarding the bell, the hallway remained motionless.

"Get to your assigned classroom," the principal and security guard yelled walking through the hall minimizing the traffic.

PJ snatched me by the arm, and we headed in the opposite direction. "Arianna, I love you! We're going to catch up as soon as school is out!"

She waved goodbye standing in the same spot. I waved back until I was around the corner, no longer able to see her.

"Who was that lame?" PJ asked concerned. We were away from the chaos.

"Don't talk about her, PJ," I stated firmly.

"Okay, whatever. Look, I'm coming to your lunch, and you can tell me about shorty then." PJ stated yet pausing, awaiting my response or reaction.

"Okay, I love you." I responded.

"I love you too." He shot back walking toward his classroom.

***

Damn, everyone must've had C lunch. This cafeteria looked like the auditorium on the first day of school. I stood at the back waiting for PJ, hoping to see Arianna. Arianna and I were like sisters, literally. We had been through so much and seeing her after all these years brought back all the horrible memoires left behind when I left that house. I wondered if Ariana was still putting up with the bullshit. She didn't deserve it.

Most would think she's eccentric and slow but she's not. After being misused and abused you don't know who to trust so you fear those around you. Me and Arianna were close. I know the real her. She had a voice that'll send chills down your spine; to me she sounded like a modern-day Fantasia.

"Kadejah!" PJ yelled standing in the entrance of the chow hall. I backpedaled out of the cafeteria while I surveyed the place through squinted eyes. "Come on, man, who you looking for?" PJ asked once I got in arm's reach.

"Quit questioning me. I'm the oldest and I'm looking for Arianna." I explained. PJ just stood there shaking his head while rolling his eyes. I couldn't expect him to understand the love and loyalty I had for Arianna when I never informed him on my past. Me and PJ were pretty close, and I didn't want to upset him with my honesty. In order for PJ to accept her I would have to tell him everything. I just hope he'll be ready to hear it.

Me and PJ were reaching for the side door when I spotted Arianna coming out of the restroom. She almost bumped into me as she strolled down the hallway, peering down, using her hands to smooth the wrinkles out of her shirt.

"Arianna!" I yelled in an attempt to gain her attention.

"Hey, Dejah!" She waved with a smile that quickly faded once she spotted PJ.

"This your lunch?" I asked, wrapping one arm around her shoulders.

"Yes, I was on my way to the cafeteria," she responded looking down at the tile floor.

"Cool. Come with us," I stated leading the way. Arianna looked up at me with uncertainty in her eyes. "It's all good, Arianna, we'll be right back." I assured as we made our way out the door and off the school property. The three of us mobbed to the corner store on the left. There was a Church's Chicken across the street.

"Man, it's hot as hell out here." PJ hailed.

Arianna and I were in deep conversation when a boy who appeared to be a few years older than me walked up, shaking up the dice that were in his left hand. He was handsome. Tall, caramel skin, nice build with deep, dark eyes. He was dressed in designers. I assumed his school didn't require uniform attire or perhaps he wasn't in school at all. I looked past him at the few others who were huddled up in a circle shooting dice. I didn't mind a little side-betting, but I didn't like shooting head up. Things always got dangerous. "Aye, you shoot?" He asked with a

35

smirk on his face. I acted as if I was green to what he was asking, knowing damn well I knew the ins and outs to shooting dice. Lil' Tim had taught me all about it. "Dice, girl. Craps. Whatever you want to call it. What about your boyfriend?" He asked pointing at PJ.

"Nah, I'm cool," PJ responded, never denying the dude's assumption.

"Well, what ab—"

"Oh, nah, she slow," PJ interjected as he chuckled loudly.

"Shut up, PJ! Come on," I shouted looking over his shoulder.

"Deja, I want to go back to school," Arianna whispered as she stood beside me, watching the guys talk shit and roll the dice.

"Okay, just give me a few minutes and then we'll go get something to eat from Church's and head back to school." I assured, trying my best to calm her spirit. I could tell by the shakiness in her voice Arianna was scared.

"Kadejah, why you treating her like she's a baby? Let her go back by her damn self." PJ commented looking at Arianna in disgust.

"Say PJ, bruh, this my last time telling you. Respect my mind, man. This my fam." I stated inching closer to PJ.

"Cool. I see how it is." PJ surrendered scowling at Arianna and me.

"Lil' mama, you ready?" Sosa asked, smirking at the other guys that were already kneeled.

I removed the fourteen dollars from my purse and squatted. "Hold this, Arianna," I stated, smoothing the wrinkles out of the crumbled bills. "T-lee?" I asked, picking up one of dice.

Sosa tossed his dice and it landed on three. Mine landed on four. "It's on you, lil' mama." He said.

"I know," I shot back, picking up the dice and shaking them up. *Snap!* "Fo-Fo' in the doe!" I yelled. "Want to bet on the four?" I asked, looking up for a split second at a shocked Sosa.

"Yeah, bet three." He was in slight awe, yet he kept his eyes on the ground.

I dropped the three bills onto the ground with a quickness. "Watch I hit again," I taunted while I looked at him with a smirk. I sideways tossed the dice like I watched Lil' Tim do so many times. "Lil' Joe!" I chanted, snatching the five dollars from the pot.

"Come on. Do it again." He dared with a smile, laying down his money.

Snap! "Big Ben!"

"I got five you don't hit that ten," he challenged.

"I got ten, boy," I shot back seriously.

"Oh, I like you," he retorted, placing the ten-dollar bill in the pot.

I shook the dice and tossed them to the ground. *Snap!* "Benjamin! I told you! You got to finesse 'em," I stated enthused.

"Come on, I ain't done," he stated. His smile had vanished and was replaced with a more focused expression. Sosa dropped his two dollars and raised up off his knee into a low squat. *Snap!*

"Nina! Watch her, she gone bang!" I teased. "Wanna bet?" I asked Sosa with a cocky smile on my face.

"Bet five," he stated.

"Bet ten," I challenged, holding up the ten-dollar bill.

"Come on. I ain't scared." He shot back throwing the ten-dollar bill on top of the pile.

I softly blew on the dice before shaking them. I was a little nervous, but I wasn't scared. *Snap!* "Nino Brown! Run me my loot!" I yipped, snatching up my money.

Sosa turned his lips downward like the head Mafia guy who sits at the end seat of the round table. "You got it, lil' mama. I underestimated you. You really tricked me on the cool!" He stated flirtatiously.

"I didn't trick you, you tried to get over on me, thinking I was green to this shit 'cause I'm a female." I calmly replied, counting my money.

"Aye! Lil' Mama!" A guy shouted from behind. He had been posted up at the store watching the dice game from a distance.

"What's up?" I asked curiously.

"Shoot ten, bet ten." He suggested, pulling a wad of cash out of his pocket.

"Nah, maybe next time I got to head back to school." I responded, tucking my cash into my bra.

"You in middle school!" He capped. "Yo, Sosa, you let a bitch in middle school take your money?" He laughed holding his stomach.

"Nigga, watch your mouth," PJ snapped.

"Nigga, who you calling a bitch?" I asked, taken back by his disrespect. Arianna grabbed my hand in an attempt to pull me away.

"You talking like you gon' do some 'bout it, bitch." He teased.

I snatched my hand away from Arianna, and before I could react, PJ had charged the dude like a mad man, swinging wildly at him. The dude side stepped the two punches and counter punched PJ with two jabs to the face, dropping PJ, sending him face first into the concrete. I could tell by the way dude clowned me and my age that he was much older, but I didn't give a damn.

"Man, Meech, you tripping. That lil' nigga in middle school!" Sosa yelled.

Arianna flew from around Sosa and leaped on Meech's back as she used her arms in an attempt to choke Meech from behind. Unfortunately, she was too flimsy to do so. He effortlessly flung her off of him and Arianna's puny body toppled onto the gravel where her head bounced off the uneven curb, instantly knocking her unconscious. Immediately after Ariana hit the ground, I was within arm's reach with my blade to his face.

"Aaaaagggrhh!" He howled in pain as I dragged my blade from the right side of his temple to his bottom lip. He tightly gripped his face to ease the burning sensation from the filthy blade. I continued to slash at his face, armpit, and chest with no remorse until I felt hands lift me off my feet and tackle me to the ground.

CHAPTER 4
DONK

I quickly swerved into the empty parking spot at the kid's school. I was on my way to check out the new spot when I got a call from the school's principal telling me to come ASAP, it's an emergency.

Several police cars were parked in front of the school which instantly sent chills down my spine as I thought about my little man and baby girl. Even though Kadejah was my sister Quaylo's first born, she was later adopted. For some odd reason Quaylo abandoned Kadejah at birth, therefore she ended up in a foster home. She was discovered by Bre and Mun. Once we got everything legit on our end, we made it official. Since Bre and Mun's death, Kadejah hadn't been out of my sight.

I entered the building and spotted Kadejah cuffed outside of the principal's office. The sight broke my heart into a thousand pieces. The last thing in this world I wanted was for Kadejah to be taken away from me, and technically she was all the family I had left.

"What's going on?" I frantically asked looking from the officer to Kadejah. Her head hung low as if she were ashamed.

"Calm down, sir." The officer stated with his arms outstretched in front of me.

"Man, don't touch me! I'll calm down when y'all tell me what's going on with my baby!" My veins protruded from my neck. My breathing ceased as I anticipated the officer's response. *I can't lose Kadejah. Not my baby*, I thought.

"She's going to juvenile for aggravated assault with a deadly weapon. She was caught cutting a young man several times in multiple areas at the gas station across the street from the school."

"Kadejah, you did what?" I asked astounded, mentally denying everything the officer claimed she was guilty of, while placing my hand over my heart.

"Uncle Donk, he hit PJ and hurt him, and knocked my foster sister Arianna unconscious. I couldn't fight him; he was too big. I'm sorry." She pleaded with watery eyes and trembling lips.

"You got her cuffed but where were your antennas when this shit was going down?" I stated loudly peering at the officer. "So, where's the other two?" I continued.

"Your son is the nurse's office; he's fine. The young lady was rushed to the hospital with a possible fractured skull. Sir, if everything was recorded and this guy lashed out like she says, you all have nothing to worry about; she'll be out in no time. In the meantime, I have to take her into custody." He announced.

My nostrils flared as I tried my best to withhold my anger. Someone was going to answer for this, and I wouldn't be returning home until they did so. "Look, baby girl." I squatted next to her as I spoke softly. "These men going to take you somewhere. You going to be safe. I'll come and pick you up in a few days."

"Unc, I understand where I'm going. I'm cognizant of the fact I did something wrong, but according to your laws, I didn't. You said one fight, we all fight, and if someone starts something it's our duty to finish it. Just promise me you'll fight for my freedom every day until I'm free."

I lowered my head as I pinched the bridge of my nose. "Look, mama, I'm not mad. I would've done what you did. I'm going to do everything in my power to get you home."

She looked up at me with glossy red eyes and raised her brows as if she was expecting to hear something else. "You didn't promise me, Uncle Donk," she stated. Kadejah knew she was in big trouble; she just needed to hear my reassuring words to carry the heavy burden that had been placed on her shoulder.

"I promise, baby girl," I vowed planting a kiss on her forehead.

"Right this way!" The policemen directed Kadejah, helping her out of the seat.

I tilted my head back, sticking my hands to the bottom of my pockets as I watched the officers escort Kadejah out of the building. She continuously glanced over her shoulders at me on the way out the door. Tears silently fell from my eyes and I decided to not follow her out, because I didn't have the strength to say goodbye twice, so I hung around in the hallway until the squad car was out of sight. I removed my phone from my pocket and called Lil' Tim.

"What up doe?" He answered coolly.

"Aye, Kadejah in trouble. I need you to find out what happened and who was involved in the incident at the Exxon on Bruton an hour ago," I pressed.

"She what? Where is she?" Lil' Tim inquired, obviously upset. Him and Kadjeah had a bond no one else could come between and he loved her wholeheartedly.

"I'll give you details later, just handle that and meet me at the house."

"Bet."

I turned away on my heels to leave, and spotted PJ coming down the hallway. I was so distraught; I had forgot PJ was in the nurse's office. His once stain-free and crisp Polo shirt was now stained with dry blood and oil streaks. The sight of PJ struck me like lightening and deeply crushed my heart. I didn't know what to say or how to feel. Wrinkles formed across my forehead as I looked at him unbelievingly.

"I tried, Donk," PJ mumbled once he was face to face with me.

"You did good, little man. Are you alright?" I asked wrapping my arm around PJ.

Tears streamed down his face. "I failed. I was supposed to protect her. Where is Kadejah? Is she in jail?" PJ continued, looking at me with a terrified expression.

"Yeah, she won't be in there long though," I mumbled feeling defeated.

"She was only trying to help. Where is Arianna?" PJ asked abruptly.

"Who?" I asked confused.

"Arianna. She was with us. Kadejah said Arianna was family. She tried to help but was hurt pretty bad in the process."

41

"Oh, yeah, she's at the hospital," I replied after thinking about what the officer and I discussed.

"Would you please take me to go see her?" PJ asked with pleading eyes.

"You knew her too?" I asked PJ, taken back by his concern.

"Not really. Actually, I was very rude to her and I feel bad now because she got hurt trying to help me. She told Kadejah not to shoot dice and go back to school, but neither of us listened." He explained. "Well, we only went to get something to eat. On the way, these dudes approached Kadejah. He thought she would be an easy target, but Kadejah ends up taking all his money and the older dude calls Kadejah the B word."

"Then what?" I interrogated, immersed to every word that escaped his lips.

"I ran toward him, swinging, and he ducked and hit me twice, making me fall and hit the cement. Arianna jumped on his back. He slung her off and her head bounced off the curb, knocking her out. That's when Dejah ran over there and start slicing him up. I kept yelling stop but she wouldn't, and soon the police arrived." PJ revealed, looking as depressed as a heartbroken woman.

I was so enraged I couldn't think straight, but at least I did know what really happened. If Kadejah cut dude as bad as the officer made it seem, then he would be in the hospital as well. "Come on. Let's go see about Arianna."

The ride to the hospital was prompt and soundless as I contemplated ways to extact revenge and get Kadejah out of her trouble. I stopped with just one foot dangling out of the car when I realized something. "Aye, PJ, what's Arianna last name?" I asked peering over my shoulder at a distressed PJ.

"I don't know," he whispered.

"Come on," I stated, hopping out of my burgundy and cream Denali truck. With hunched shoulders PJ trailed behind me. "Aye, man, pick ya head up and stick ya chest out, it's gon' be alright." I stated, brushing his fade with the palm of my hand. The hospital reeked of baby poop, throw up and bleach. I looked around at all of the people that waited in the lobby. I hated hospitals. The paintings looked cheap, and most of the paint on the walls were peeling. I made a mental note for me and my family to go somewhere else for medical attention if Dr. Hayes wasn't available. As I inched closer to the desk, I noticed the woman sitting behind it was arguing with someone on the other end of the phone. *It's always a black bitch being unprofessional*, I thought. "Excuse me," I invoked.

She spun around, peered up at me and ended the call without warning the party on the other end. "Yes, how can I help you, sir?" She inquired, batting her eyelashes.

"My niece was involved in an accident at school and was brought in with a head injury about 30 to 35 minutes ago." I informed.

"Oh, yes, I remember. What's her name again?" She asked eyeing me like she was a lion and I was the piece of steak.

"Arianna," I announced.

"Arianna what? She pried.

"Look." I paused, peeling a hundred-dollar bill off the top, sliding it across the counter. "I'm just here with my son to see his cousin. They were involved in the same accident. She just ended up with the shorter end of the stick." I convinced.

She quickly snatched up the hundred-dollar bill like I knew she would. "I'm only asking because her father is in there right now." She revealed.

"Okay, my son just wants to see her real quick." I assured.

"Okay, well since I'm doing you a favor, can I have one?" She asked. She was actually kind of cute, but ratchet. Her almond colored skin was covered with her pink scrubs. Her hair was loosely pinned up and a few curls hung loosely. Here lashes were thick, I couldn't tell if they were hers or mink. Brows were on fleek which enhanced her tight, chinky eyes, and even though she had a small gap, her teeth were straight and white.

"What's up?"

"Can I get your number?" She boldly asked.

I quickly scribbled my number down on the sign-in paper, making a mental note to question her about anyone else that came in around the same time Arianna did, but with stab wounds.

"Thank ya. Room 104," she responded cheerfully, placing the sheet of paper inside her bra.

"Come on," I told PJ, pushing him toward the corridor that led to the patient rooms. I didn't even know Arianna, but I love whoever my kids love. PJ and I walked side by side, fast pacing like we were on a mission.

"104!" he shouted.

"Ssshh. Don't just burst in, she's probably sleeping." I voiced.

PJ slowly twisted the nob before pushing it open, and the sight in plain view made my stomach turn.

"What the fuck?" I mouthed with my eyes squinted in total disbelief.

Arianna's foster father had one hand tightly clasped over her mouth; it muffled the sound. His other hand moved swiftly and forcefully back and forth under Arianna's gown. "This your way of escaping from me?" He asked Arianna, not even realizing he had company.

Before I could react, PJ attacked him like a lion trying to protect his cubs. The foster father lifted his hands to protect his face.

Enraged at the sight of his middle and ring finger covered in blood, I swiftly turned around and locked the door. *Clink!* The sharp sound caused my head to swivel. Arianna's foster father laid motionless, slumped against the wall with just a corner of blood that never trickled, not even a little, but remained stagnant in the middle of his forehead. Arianna sobs had ceased, and PJ looked down at his victim with a wide-eyed expression.

"Don't panic," were the first words to escape my mouth. I looked around the small room frantically thinking about my next move. I surveyed the room, inspecting the crime scene. Not only did I have a dead man on my hands, but Arianna's gown and sheets were covered in blood. Her knees we're pulled into her chest and she looked frightened.

"Donk wha—"

Knock! Knock! The knock at the door caused PJ to pause mid-sentence. I looked from him to Arianna, placing a finger in front of my lips. I dragged the lifeless body into the restroom and closed the door. Clean sheets rested on the shelf. I quickly grabbed one and threw it on top of Arianna before opening the door.

"Yes." I welcomed, low key not wanting to invite her in.

"Hey, I was on my lunch break and stopped by to make sure everything was okay. You're only allowed a thirty-minute visit." She informed, peeking her head in.

"Yeah, we're wrapping things up. 'Preciate ya," I replied, easing the door closed.

She put her hand out to prevent the door from closing. "You hungry?" she asked.

"Nah, we good," I responded dryly, growing impatient. She blew me a kiss and strutted down the hall. I quickly shut the door and began wiping down everything with one of the clean towels. "Arianna, can you walk?" I asked, steady wiping.

PJ helped her down off the bed, but as soon as her feet touched the tile floor, her knees buckled, causing her to lose her balance.

I slid the window open and looked from left to right. "PJ, go first and make sure the coast is clear for me and Arianna to go."

"Ok," he responded. I could hear the hint of fear in his voice.

I cradled Arianna in my arms and looked around the room one last time.

PJ slowly climbed out the window, watching his surroundings carefully. "Come on, Donk," he rushed with his eyes trained for any sudden movement.

I turned sideways and effortlessly climbed out of the window, using one hand to close and lock it behind me. As soon as I bypassed a few more windows to the other rooms, I noticed my truck was still illegally parked in front of the entrance. Two to three onlookers spotted me, but it was no turning back now. I opened the backdoor carefully placing Arianna in the backseat. I hopped in and peeled off.

Ah'Million

CHAPTER 5
PERSUASIA

"Ooooohhhhh! Bitch, I like this," Esha said, holding up the gold trimmed cheetah print body suite.

"Bitch, that look like something I'll walk around in before hitting the stage." I joked as I continued rummaging through the clothes on the rack.

Esha and I had been friends for years. I actually met Esha my senior year of high school. We were both on the drill team for Roosevelt High School. Thick as thieves neither one of us were very fortunate nor were our parents, so we boosted clothes from the malls, outlets, flea markets and phones from electronic stores. We used our good looks and banging bodies to attract dope boys and jack boys, when we discovered our passion for dancing. Instead of making twerk video for free, we decided to make cash for shaking ass. Esha still dances to this day. The plan was to just dance for our tuition fees, but she fell in love with the lifestyle.

Esha put you in the mind of a ratchet version of Trina. The only difference was Esha had a small, flat mole in the middle of her top lip, her ass was bigger, and she had a dermal piercing on the far side under her left eye. Esha loved to dance, she performed more than anything. She did more pole tricks than ass clapping and a lot of people came out to see her. When I was dancing, me and Esha would hit the stage and they called us milk and honey. We would do this one move that will make a working man throw his whole wallet on stage. Esha would climb all the way up. I'll grip the pole extremely tight with my legs and lean back, feet straight ahead, leveling my body resembling an ironing board. Esha would straighten her bent knees allowing them to lightly land on my stomach. She'd release her grip on the pole and balance herself on top of me, moving her arms in a motion like a surfer. Before I know it, I'm walking out the club with three Hefty trash bags. Thinking back on days like that occasionally made me miss the club, but the love I had for Donk made those thoughts vanish. Donk was the type of dude you spend your whole life with, if you were given the opportunity. He was the perfect man. He excelled sexually, took care of home and my expensive taste, treated my son like his blood ran through him, and he treats me with the upmost respect as if I'm the only woman in the world.

"This is me right here." I stated lifting the dress over the rack so Esha could get a better view.

"Oh, yeah, I like that. Donk going to kill you, bitch!" She taunted, staring at the dress, nodding her head in approval.

The burgundy and gold, sleeveless dress hugged my curves perfectly. The back of it was cut out in the shape of a diamond that stopped just above my butt. The gold chain that connected from one side to the other fell perfectly above my breast. The dress barely covered my butt cheeks, but it was so sexy I didn't mind tugging at the bottom of it all night. It wasn't like we were going to a club, it was just close friends getting together enjoying ourselves at an elegant restaurant.

Bzzzzz! Bzzzzz! Bzzzz! I laid the dress across my arm while I retrieved my phone from my purse. "Hey, Bae!" I answered enthused. "What? I'm on my way!" I yelled, immediately ending the call as I quickly threw the dress over the rack. "Come on, Esha," I called out, exiting the store.

"What about your dress?" she yelled.

I didn't even bother to respond.

***

Donk's car was parked in the driveway when I arrived at the house. I thought about taking Esha home, but I needed details ASAP. My hands were shaking uncontrollably and I had dropped the keys a few times in an attempt of getting inside the house. "Donk! Baby!" I called out as I looked around frantically.

"I'm in the study!" He yelled.

"Everything okay, Persuasia? Take a deep breath, honey," Esha lightly spoke full of concern.

Without responding to Esha I sprinted toward Donk's study. I didn't even take the time to remove my heels. I could see the worry in his eyes. I grabbed him by the face and kissed his lips. "Tell me what's going on," I stated while gazing into his eyes.

"The kids got into a fight. Long story short, Kadejah ran into her foster sister whom was with them as well. Kadejeah ends up cutting the dude so she's taken to juvy. The sister who name is Arianna suffered a head concussion. In the midst of that, PJ tells me he wants to check on her progression, so I take him to the hospital. When we walk into her room, the foster father is there and raping her, however he's using his fingers to do the job. PJ attacks him, I turn to lock the door, turn back around and dude is dead. From there, we snuck out of the room." Donk explained.

"Dontrail, are you serious?" I asked in disbelief, gripping my head in frustration. "Where's PJ?" I questioned in shock.

"Come on," Donk demanded, grabbing my hand as he led the way. Donk opened the door to PJ's room. Arianna rested peacefully on his bed in one of his Polo pajama sets. PJ set in a chair next to the bed, carefully stroking her hair as the tears fell silently.

Who is she? I thought. *How did they get so close? I never witnessed PJ being so attentive.* I walked toward the bed, snapping PJ out of his trance, looking down at Arianna. She looked a bit rough around the edges, but she was beautiful. Her curly hair was pulled up into a ponytail and her smooth cappuccino adore skin possessed a glow. Her thick eyebrows had a natural arch, but you could tell they had never been touched. "Come here, PJ," I whispered. He followed me out of the bedroom. "PJ, how did that guy die at the hospital?" I asked.

PJ looked up at Donk who stood behind the with his hands in his pockets. "I was punching him, then he tried to grab me. He had blood on his hands which allowed me to slip away from his grasp and I shoved him. Once I did that, he lost his balance and made direct contact with the railing of the bed." PJ explained. "I didn't know he could easily die from a slip and fall. Ma, it happened so fast. I just tried to help Arianna like she helped me." He spoke in between sniffles.

"PJ, I'm here. You gon' be okay. Whenever you got me, and I have breath in my body, you have nothing to worry about." Donk stated before walking away.

CHAPTER 6
KADEJAH

The stench of the tiny room had me dizzy. The smell put me in the mind of an old auditorium, moth balls and corn chips all in one. The toilet was positioned in the corner of the wall. It was full of piss and toilet paper. There were no windows, but I could see a bright light seeping underneath the door. After what felt like hours, I'd finally awoke drenched in sweat. It was a nightmare from hell, despite the fact it was a blast from the past. Nothing fabricated about the vivid flick inside of my mind.

"Come on!" The female officer announced as she stood in the doorway.

I quickly rose to my feet and walked out of the room. After going through the testing procedure, the officer made me wash, rinse and air dry my hair. I stripped out of the uniform I had on and into the juvenile clothes which were navy blue scrubs. I walked down the long hallway with fear seeping out of my pores. My hair was matted down like old carpet. We were granted hygiene bags the size of a small Ziploc bag that contained a hotel size deodorant, five white bars of soap the size of dominoes, toothpaste, four ounce bottle of cocoa butter lotion, toothbrush and a flimsy purple comb. She removed the large keys from her pocket and opened a door that had a big G on it. An antique 20-inch TV decorated the shelf. About ten chairs were lined up in rows of two. I peered around at the girls who all seemed to be into the show until they spotted me. Some were mugging and some just stared at me.

"You in cell six. Go put your things up. It's fresh linen to make the bed, then come back out and take you a seat." She stated, closing the door behind her.

"Yes, ma'am," I replied, walking to cell six.

By passing the girls I heard a few whispers. "Where you from? This your first time?" They asked but I ignored them.

The room was small with bunkbeds. I assumed my bed was the one that wasn't made. I sat my hygiene bag on the table and went over to my bed which was only two to three feet away. I looked at the bed on the lower bunk and mimicked it as best I could. I walked out of the cell, closing the door behind me, causing the girls to turn their heads in my direction. I sat down in the first empty seat I saw. I sat directly across from a girl who resembled a boy in a feminine way though. I sort of looked longer than what I was supposed to, only because she looked familiar. Which I later found out we attended the same elementary school; she was considered a cool kid. I wasn't.

Her eyes are what really caught my attention. They were the color of Krispy Kreme glazed donuts, without the glaze of course. Her hair was braided very tiny and neat into three layers. The small gaps in between a few of her teeth unmasked her innocence. She was what you referred to as a red bone. From the looks of it I could tell she didn't hear that phrase being used to refer to her too often.

"Kadejah, we're done with phone calls for the day, but I'll let you make a call after I rack everyone up." The officer announced. Her name was Ms. Smith. Ms. Smith looked very simple but pretty. She had nice lengthy jet-black hair that was pulled into a low ponytail. She was paper sack brown with butt and hips for days. Her lips were noticeably darker than her skin color, so I assumed she smoked weed.

"Yes, ma'am," I quickly responded, relieved to hear some good news.

"Aye, what's yo' name?" The girl across from me asked.

"Kadejah," I replied looking down at my fingers.

"I'm Tru. What you in here for?" She asked eagerly, never looking away.

"Tru, like, Truuu?" I questioned, imitating the rapper Two Chainz.

"Yeah, like that." She smiled.

"I'm in here for aggravated assault," I revealed, still looking down at my fingers.

"What?" Her eyes grew to the size of golf balls, not to mention they were naturally quite bigger than most.

"Man, you'll be alright." One of the girls in the row behind me intervened.

"Yeah, you can still go home with a charge like that. I have the same charge," the chick said.

"How long have you been here?" I asked curiously. "My name is Kadejah, by the way," I continued.

"I'm Shun and that's Kedra." Shun was the color of an oat-meal pie. The blackheads on her face made her resemble one too. Her hair was about four inches long, all the same length, yet nappy and bridle. Her teeth were perfect like she'd worn braces all her life.

Kedra looked mixed but I looked at the texture of her hair and assumed she was full Negro. Her hair was styled in an afro and it was a tad bit shorter than Shun's. Her lips were pink and succulent, and she had deep brown eyes and a beautiful smile. A little unusual to admit, but she looked like a female version of the rapper Chingy. Kedra and Shun were a little hype. I heard them behind me quoting songs from rappers J Dawg and Webbie. I wanted to chime in, but I was so terrified at the reality of it all.

I missed my uncle and little brother. I know Lil' Tim would be highly upset once he finds out, not so much with me but with the guy who disrespected me. Lil' Tim was very overprotective of me. Some days after riding and hanging with him all day, I would go home and daydream about us being together, even though I knew it would never happen. I had a crush on Lil' Tim since I was old enough to know what a crush was.

"So, what happened?" Shun asked interrupting me from my thoughts.

I looked at her then at Tru and then back at Kedra. I felt the back of my eye sockets burn right before the tears fell down my face. I began replaying the events calmly and slowly, but as I recanted loudly I became mystical; the tone in my voice elevated and my left leg shook uncontrollably as I continued on explaining. They all looked at me with pitiful and concerned expressions as I brought the detective's words to surface.

"Oh, if your lawyer said they're pushing for self-defense then that's what it's going to be. It sound like self-defense to me." She commented.

I turned my head and made unintentional eye contact with Tru. It looked like something was bothering her, but she stayed silent.

"Damn, you gangsta!" Kedra interjected, staring at me in astonishment.

"Fox 4 news at eight, breaking news!" The TV roared loudly as Ms. Smith increased the volume. Everyone got quiet and focused in on the TV screen. It went from sounding like a gym during P.E. class to the moment of silence part after you recite the pledge of allegiance. "I'm Tammy and this is your Fox 4 news report. A thirteen-year-old female was taken into custody and is now at the Henry Wade Juvenile Detention Center charged with aggravated assault with deadly weapon. The attack took place at Exxon gas station On Bruton Road. The suspect, Kadejah Richards, was skipping school at the time. Her and a few more students attending Florence Middle School. The victim allegedly threatened the suspect which resulted in her attack. The suspect slashed the victim over ten times. Officers arrived and restrained her immediately."

A mugshot of me popped up on the screen and everyone but Tru looked at me. I could tell she wanted to look as well. She had been discreetly cutting her eyes at me while keeping her head straight. I knew the shit was hurting her eyes. I used to do the same thing when I would be in the car with Lil Tim while he handled business.

"The victim, 22 years old Kory Matthewsd, is currently hospitalized. No life-threatening injuries at this moment."

I smirked deviously as they showed the victim. *Kory had no business in our business at twenty-two years old*, I thought. I knew he was older by his facial hair, but I didn't know he was that much older. He had no right laying a finger on PJ, especially not the way he did. I should've cut that motherfucker off. Better yet, I should've off his ass.

"We'll be back with more of your Fox 4 news report."

All the girls started whispering among themselves while sneaking glances at me. I didn't notice that I never removed the smirk off my face until I looked over and saw Tru looking at me with look of uncertainty plastered across her face, and I met her gaze before dropping my head in embarrassment.

Ah'Million

CHAPTER 7
LIL' TIM

I rapped along to Young Dolph's new hit *Major* as I bobbed my head to the beat. I swerved into the Barbershop's lot, killed the engine then hopped out the whip.

"Aye, I'm at the barbershop taking care of somethin', but in 'bout ten minutes I need you to meet me at Peach's spot," I informed Bando. "The one on Colonial," I responded hanging up. I opened the door to the barbershop and immediately scanned the place for my boy Scoop. We called him Scoop 'cause he knew everything that went on in the hood. The time, location, and temperature if you ask. Despite the fact he stayed a couple blocks from the barbershop he had the scoop on shit from the East to the Nawf, the Grove to the Cliff. He even knew a thing or two around Mesquite and Garland.

"Aye, yo E! Is Scoop somewhere around here?" I asked. E was part owner of the barbershop and had the skills to pay the bills. You go sit in his chair, you leaving with something that resemble a hundred dollar lining.

"Yeah, fam, he in the back. Got-damn! Where you been, nigga? I ain't saw you in about two weeks!" He exclaimed, cutting the clippers off while we fist pumped.

"Nigga, it ain't been two weeks! Some shit done came up with my lil' shorty and I got to get some answers, E." I confided in a low tone, not wanting none of the grimy ass dudes who sat observing our encounter in our business.

"Oh yeah! Well that nigga in the back!" Before I could walk away, E tugged me backwards by my shoulder and whispered, "Let me know if I can help in anyway, nigga. You know how we do."

E went from cutting hair out of his garage to a nice establishment. Martin Luther King Jr. and Malcolm X paintings decorated the wall, as well as Lebron James, Wilt Chamberlain, Kyrie Irving and Bill Russell portraits in the mix. The different decors resembled the establishment on the movie *Barbershop*. Bright lights, real niggas and a lot of cash and high-siding, or talking shit. We called it the Spot.

I bypassed a few dudes sitting on the sectional toward the back, playing Madden on the plasma waiting to get faded. A few were already faded. Focusing back on the task at hand, I barely caught the glimpse of the familiar face which immediately made me stop dead in my tracks. My eyes lingered longer than they should've. Dude wasn't even paying me any attention. However, I couldn't place exactly where I knew dude from. I headed on toward the back in a slow pace, steady trying to rack my brain. I hated when something was on the tip of my tongue, yet I still couldn't taste it.

"Lil' Tim, what's up, nigga?" Chris shouted, sitting at the poker table with a cigar hanging out of his mouth as he waved me over. The back of the spot was a gambling shack. Several tables occupied the spacious area. Spade table, Domino table, Tonk, Pitty-pad, Deuces Wild and a massive dice game going on in the far corner.

"What's up, baby?" I spoke in a nonchalant tone.

Chris instantly picked up on my vibe. "Nigga, you good?" He questioned. His smile faded and his expression was now humorless and savage as he quickly removed his Cartier glasses.

"Man, some nigga done got at Donk little ones and I'm tryin' to get some answers 'cause I'm 'bout ready to start shooting shit up."

"Scoop?" Chris called out, searching the room. Scoop was dark skinned with a mouth full of golds. He stood 5'9" and tattoos covered his arms. He had a real slim build; the wind would blow Scoop's ass away if it was too windy outside. The chicks loved his thin ass.

"What's up, fam? Tim, how long you been up here?" Scoop asked, quickly scanning my eyes.

"I just got up here, looking for you. Man, I need some info." I stated distressed.

"What's up? Quit looking crazy, nigga, and rap."

"It was some shit went down at the Exxon on Burton earlier. You know anything about it?"

"The youngins and the dice game?" Scoop asked with a puzzled expression.

"Yeah, what happened?" I inquired.

"They say some underage kids were skipping school trying to shoot dice, a chick hit one of the lil' cats for nearly everything in his pocket, so Meech was up there posted and tried to get in the dice game, but lil' mama start popping off. Meech got lit, a young nigga with the chick rushed Meech, Meech dropped him, dragged another chick, and the fly chick sliced his ass up with a blade; almost killed him," Scoop explained.

"Ha Ha Ha! Hell yeah. I saw that shit. Meech ass is a trip. He dropped lil' dude so quick I had to rub my eyes to see if I was tripping. That shit was hilarious." A guy who was seated at the poker table added.

"Oh, that's funny?" I asked with the meanest scowl a nigga could muster. Before he could respond, I snatched the .40 from my waist and slapped dude across his jaw. As the iron connected with his pearly whites, they crumbled and shattered. I bashed his mouth in a few more times before wrapping my free hand around his throat. I wanted him to choke on every tooth I knocked out his mouth.

"Aye, back the fuck up before I start bustin' motherfuckas! Innocent motherfuckas and all, back up!" Chris yelled, hovering beside me.

"Tim, come on, don't kill him, man. The spot already hot." E called out.

E's words snapped me back into reality. I instantly removed my hands and tucked the burner back inside my jeans. I could tell by E's expression that I wore a fiendish scowl.

"Lil' Tim, gone go handle your business, I'll get this shit cleaned up."

"Bet," I responded, walking through the crowd that my wrath caused to form. Despite all the dudes in my path, I still noticed dude in the corner, although this time he was watching my every move. Time wasn't on my side. I'll just have to deal with him later.

Click! Clack! I looked toward the door of the barbershop and spotted Bando with a composed yet deranged expression, clutching a 223 with both hands.

"Hold on, nigga, I'm good!"

"Shit! Tell me somethin'," he stated puffing on the blunt that never left his mouth. "I heard it was some shit going on and you told me you was gone stop by here, and you wasn't answering your phone, nigga!" He said still holding the automatic rifle.

"Man, come yo crazy ass on, boy. I'm damn near thirty and a nigga ain't did shit to me!" I quoted walking behind Bando as we made our exit.

"Nigga, you ain't even close to thirty!" he joked.

***

Me and Bando stepped out of our shoes as we entered Donk's home, but today the TV wasn't blaring from a NBA game nor did several dishes of food cover the table. Persuasia led us into Donk's study. I called it his man cave. I tried not to stare at her ass as she led the way, but the Fashion Nova joggers hugged every curve to perfection. Feeling the dreariness, I decided to clear my throat rather than speak to announce my presence.

Donk's head was buried in his hands, and once he finally removed them I could see the exasperation all over his face. He tightened his lips in an attempt to conceal his emotions before standing to his feet. "Tim, fuck the details, I just want a name." He voiced.

"Meech," I responded without hesitation.

"The lil' dude that be selling the nick and dimes at Big D's?" Donk questioned.

"Yeah, fam, you ready?"

Without a response Donk grabbed his Glock out of the dresser, checked the clip and proceeded out the door.

***

"Where you at, nigga?" Lil' Reggie screamed through the phone.

"It's been a change. Me, Donk and Bando on a mission," I stated as we sat patiently behind tint, waiting on Meech to return to his grandmother's house.

"Without me!" Reggie hollered.

"Yeah! This shit urgent. We gone swing through once we done." I assured becoming frustrated with Reggie's interrogation.

"Aye, I'm out here bad; my sneaks talking, nuts musty, and my ribs showing." That was the code to let me know he was running out of dope fast and needed to re-up immediately.

"Bet," I stated before ending the call. Donk turned the AC up in the duck off while waiting for Meech. "So, fam, what they saying about Kadejah?" I asked.

"They trying to hit her with an aggravated assault with deadly weapon. I called Steve earlier; he on it right now." He responded without talking his eyes off the house.

"There that nigga go right there!" Bando yelled.

Meech wasn't even in a car. You would think at least a family member would sympathize enough to pick him up from the hospital. Meech came limping down the sidewalk; several bandages covered his arms and face. No telling how many time Kadejah actually cut him, but you could tell he was in pain. He wasn't even paying attention to the black Nissan Maxima that was parked across the street, loaded with predators who were on the hunt for prey. As soon Meech made it to the door, the blow to the back of Meech's head caused him to grip the throbbing organ and tighten the grip at the pain. Blood seeped through his fingers as he turned his head to get a look at his attacker.

"Turn yo' ass back around and unlock the door." Donk spoke through clenched teeth.

Meech turned toward the door while fidgeting with the keys. They fell to the floor twice before Donk bashed him across the head again, making Meech fall to his knees from the impact of the blow.

"Drag his ass in once I open the door," Donk stated, picking the keys up off the ground.

There was no doubt about it, this was Meech's grandmother's house. It had the old lady smell— moth balls, Pine Sol and old cigarette smoke as if she had the same furniture for years and the smoke seeped through the fabric. Different biblical quotes covered the walls in the living room. You could hear a faint sound of television in the back. Meech laid sprawled out on the floor. I returned to the living room with a jug of water to wake his ass up.

"Aaagghhh! Aaagghh! Grrhh! Mm.mhmm!" Meech hollered, swinging wildly as if he could hit the water. Immediately after realizing it was water, he quickly closed his mouth to prevent himself from choking on the liquid.

"Nigga, shut up," I demanded in a low tone, kicking Meech in his side.

Donk and Bando scanned the house to make sure we were alone. I looked down at a bloody Meech and thanked God I had moved up; I was no longer petty hustling alongside him. Me and him used to race to the cars that pulled up. I knew Meech wasn't going to amount to shit. I would save, he would buy shoes and fits to hit the club or latest party. As long as my hair was cut and I had shoes to step out in when it was time, I was good. I used to be posted on the block with the same fit for two days. Give me a V-neck or a tank top, pair of sweatpants or some Levi's, and pair of Nike's or Reebok Classics and I'm good. I made sure I had a fresh fade on every set and I smelled descent. I wasn't the type of nigga to spray cologne on funk. Once that Dolce and Gabanna Light Blue or Polo Blue wear off, it was just faint until I hit that water again. But boy, did it take a minute for it to wear off. Those two scents almost guaranteed I would get the pussy. Straight up.

Meech always shot me envious looks from the side or behind my back that he thought I didn't catch, but I did. I learned at a young age; niggas get mad when you doing good, especially when you're doing better than them. Shit, from the outside looking in, you would've thought Meech was the man with the plan. He always dressed designer head to toe, two or three chains around his neck. Unbeknownst, dude didn't have ten dollars to buy him a meal from a Church's Chicken menu. If he wanted to stunt, I let him. Time tells everything. I just tried to give him some news he could use in the mean and in between time. I knew Meech stayed with his grandmother. He would always talk about her illness and how he wanted to get her out the hood.

"Aye, it's an old lady in the back, hooked up to a breathing machine." Donk stated. He peered over at Meech devilishly, picking up the picture on top of the shelf.

"She's sick. I'm sorry man! I'm sorry! Man, my big mama dying. Please don't kill me, man, she need me!" Meech yelled in desperation, straining his neck to make eye contact with Donk.

"Where's the little girl?" Donk asked, eyeing the picture of the beautiful adolescent.

"That's my little sister; she's in the ninth grade. I suppose to pick her up from school." He panted.

"If you got all this shit going on in your life, why the fuck you put your hands on my shorty, man?" I asked sincerely through squinted eyes. I wanted so badly to put a bullet between his eyes, but because me and Meech had more than a few late-night flights, I was willing to scare him straight then let him walk away—barely walking, but breathing. I know Donk didn't feel the same.

"Come on, Tim. Man, you like a brother to me!" He whined in between sniffles.

"Nigga, don't start all that 'I'm ya brother' ass shit. We ain't even spoke since I left the block." I retorted.

Bando paced the floor. He looked as if he didn't care who died or lived at this point. Donk turned his back to me as he began to fidget with something in his hands.

"Lil' Tim…Aye, fam. Mariyah probably on her way home right now." Meech cried with fear in his eyes. I looked away to avoid eye contact. Now was not the time to sympathize.

Donk swiftly squatted beside Meech. "I'm going to offer you a deal. You can take it or leave it." Donk stated calmly as he balanced himself on the tips of his toes.

"Anything, man. I'm sorry, Donk; I am!" Meech hollered a bit relieved.

"I'm gon' take your life for fucking with my youngins, but I'm going to make sure your baby sis and grandma straight." Donk announced coldly. I should've known Donk wasn't going to give Meech ass a pass. The more I thought about Kadejah in that cold ass cell I wanted to pop his ass myself. Meech looked from me to Donk unsure of what to say. *Psst! Psst!* Before he could utter a word, Donk silenced him for good with two shots to the face. "I'll take that as a deal," Donk insisted, standing to his feet. "Come on, y'all. Let's wrap this nigga up and get out of here."

CHAPTER 8
PERSUASIA

"She took a nice bang to the head. She's lucky to be alive. She's not responsive right now; a little incoherent; but she should be back to normal in a few days to a week, maybe two weeks at the most." The doctor claimed. "As for the situation with her being molested, it caused her to lose a pretty good amount of blood. From the looks of things, he's done it more than once. I've prescribed two different types of antibiotics to prevent and cure infections, as well as soothe the swelling." Doctor Haynes had been our private doctor for years now to avoid unsanitary hospitals and nosey people. She was all about her money, but I think she had a thang for Donk.

PJ stood in the hallway listening to everything the doctor said. I watched him closely as I waited for Doctor Haynes to finish writing out the prescription.

"Call me if there's another situation," she stated, handing me the prescription. She gently rubbed PJ on the head as she passed him on the way out.

PJ slowly walked up on me with his hands in his pockets. Feeling his distress, I motioned for him to come sit next to me on the sectional. "Ma?" He called out in a low tone.

"Yes, baby?"

"Why did that old man do that to Arianna when it's so many old ladies out there?" He asked with a puzzled yet curious expression on his face.

I had never seen my son so vulnerable. "Baby, he was a de-ranged man and sick in the mind. People like that are in prison or on their way." I responded the best way I could.

"So, how long will it take for Arianna to talk again?"

"I don't know, honey, but don't worry yourself. You still have to go to school and focus on your grades. You're just a kid too."

"Yes, I understand everything you're saying, but what I do want you to know is, even if it takes her a year to utter one word, I'm going to be right here by her side until she does."

65

Caught off guard at his response I peered at PJ with a wide-eyed expression. "You love that girl, PJ? You too young to know what love is." I snapped.

"Nah, mama, I don't love her. I don't even know what love is. I'm loyal to her 'cause she was loyal to me, and I prefer loyalty over love any day 'cause love will hurt you or get you killed." With that being said PJ gave me one last look over his shoulder before going back inside his room where Arianna lay asleep.

"Where you at, chick?" I asked Esha who was on the other end of the phone.

"Chilling, getting ready to do this private show; me and Hennessy." She said.

"Um. You and that hoe Hennessey locked in now?"

"Bitch, you's married now, you can't come." She chuckled into the phone.

"Where's it at?" I asked nonchalantly.

"Out in the boondocks. Quick Rich throwing it."

"Quick Rich? The one that own club 227 with the money green Rolls Royce?" I inquired skeptically.

"Yes, bitch, and it's only going to be me and Hennessey shaking ass and popping pussy!" She yelled, obviously enthused.

I thought about how Quick Rich and his boys got down, but quickly dismissed the thought 'cause none of it compared to the things Donk did or the way he made me feel. "Well, have fun. I'm leaving Walgreen's, about to head back home," I stated.

Esha seemed a bit occupied. I could hear Hennessy's laughter in the background as I pictured them half naked, with every beauty product you can imagine placed on the counter while they stood in front of the bathroom or vanity mirror prepping themselves for tonight's event. I squared all the way up, but I'm not going to lie, there are days that I miss those nights. The Kush in the air, liquor in my system; not to much but just enough to have me feeling tipsy while I talked shit, turned up on the latest music and got ready to hit the stage.

"Alright, girl, I'll call you tomorrow once I sober up. I love you!" She quipped just before ending the call.

I was never fond of Hennessey. She used to always try and take my regulars at the club, but I guess she didn't get the memo. Once you go Persuasia, you don't want no other flavor. I laughed to myself as I pulled into the driveway. PJ really alarmed me with his choice of words earlier. I needed to make a mental note to discuss with Donk exactly what he told me, 'cause I know he could've heard such things from no one else but Donk. Which was the truth no doubt. Some days I wondered if PJ will remember those days I abandoned him to go work at the club.

PJ was back in the spot he was in when I first got wind of the incident. Only now he was fast asleep. I walked over to the love seat, removed his sneakers and his hat, and covered him up with a thin blanket. I started to awake Arianna so she could take her pills but decided against it. I sat the prescription next to the bed and tip toed out of the room.

Ah'Million

CHAPTER 9
DONK

I lost the building to another buyer. I had other shit to worry about. Steve had yet to call me about any new information regarding Kadejah's case, but I'd put money on Steve. He made shit happen. Lil' Tim and Bando hopped back in his whip and headed into the opposite direction to hook up with Lil' Reggie. Reggie was my guy, Bando's was Lil' Tim.

Reggie was a dude I clicked tight with when I did my six year bid for a jewelry store robbery. I didn't fuck with them cats like that 'cause they acted like broads, but me and Reggie clicked from the jump. I first met him when we worked in the kitchen together at Beto Unit. We didn't have to steal shit 'cause he was fucking the Sergeant. The kitchen commissary Sergeant at that. Kitchen commissary is where they stored everything as a whole. We had a smooth system going on and Reggie had me holding things down, while he was knee-deep in the guts. We even snatched the handheld scale and was weighing slices of cheese and meat like we owned a Deli. Sugar, butter, milk, cinnamon, tortillas, salsa, brown sugar, seasoned salt, onions and whatever else was on the menu. Business was good before niggas start hating, but I knew that was bound to happen. Anytime you doing wrong, you have to get the getting while the getting is good, 'cause sooner or later shit turns for the worse.

They locked Reggie and I up in seg while they investigated things further. I guess we were labeled as the head honchos. The month we were back there it only felt like a week. We flirted with the female COs, cracked jokes, talked shit to the male laws, and shared stories about our life on the outside. Reggie was the exact nigga on the outside that he claimed to be when we were locked up. He just wasn't one of those dudes talking how he had this and that but didn't have shit. He was the truth.

Days like this I really missed Mun. Apart of me wanted to believe he was alive, but I know he was dead and gone 'cause it's no way in hell he would've let all this time pass without finding me.

Ring! Ring! The loud tone from my iPhone quickly caught my attention. I stared down at the screen but didn't recognize the number at all. "Wad up?" I asked smoothly.

"I didn't get your name earlier, but this the chick from the hospital. I—"

"Hey, ma, can you meet me?" I asked cutting her short.

"Yeah, where at?"

"The Braum's on St. Augustine."

"Okay, I'm about ten minutes away."

My heartbeat sped up 'cause I knew she was going to inform me on the expected. I busted an illegal U-turn at the red light and made my way to the Braum's. I dialed Persuasia's number to make sure everything at home was straight.

"Hey, daddy." She softly spoke.

"Has Kadejah called?"

"No, not yet. Are you on your way?"

"Not right now. I got something to take care of real quick."

"Okay." She sighed.

"I love you," I admitted.

"I love you too," she replied so soft I could barely hear.

I could hear the agitation in Persuasia's voice when I told her I wasn't on my way home but I didn't have time to set her straight. It amazed me how women just couldn't ride the wave. When a nigga too good they get bored and crave a little dysfunction. Just be grateful, fuck me, feed me, treat me and enjoy a nigga's presence, 'cause with the life I live, tomorrow isn't promised.

Coincidentally, I pulled into the parking spot next to shorty. She didn't even realize I was on the side of her. She sang along and bobbed her head to the beat. I killed the engine so I could hear what she was jamming. Drake and Chris Brown's *No Guidance* blared through her speakers. I hopped out the whip and swaggered over to her car. I tapped on the window where she was seated, scaring the shit out of her.

She jumped before placing her hand over her heart. "Come on, with yo' scary ass," I joked loudly, walking away.

"Boy, you scared me." She smiled, following me into the Braum's.

I walked to the counter and began scanning the menu. "Just give me a strawberry shake and a six-piece chicken tender. What you want?" I asked.

"The same." She blushed. Shorty was smiling so hard I could see all of her teeth. She was either a happy chick or really enjoyed being in a nigga's presence. I wasn't surprised, I had that effect on women.

I paid the cashier and took a seat at the table by the door. "So…What's up?"

"Okay, all bullshit to the side. A nurse found a dead body in the bathroom of the room you all were in and notified the police. Every type of law you could think of been snooping around and asking questions. I got in trouble by my boss because I couldn't produce the second visitor's name on the sign in sheet. It's clear her father was present 'cause that's the only visitor according to what's in black and white."

"So, how do they know it was more than one visitor?" I inquired.

"They reviewed the tapes." Cameras inside the hospital didn't surprise me whatsoever, but I didn't know if they monitored the activity in the rooms. I was hoping once everything came out, they wouldn't be able to decipher if PJ or myself did the hit.

"It's only a matter of time, baby. I'm sorry, we never formally introduced ourselves. I'm Mia and you are?"

"Donk," I retorted in frustration, as I made eye contact with the cashier who waved me over for the food.

Mia followed my eyes, quickly stood to her feet and strutted over to the counter. Her walk put a nigga in a trance, but I quickly shook that shit off 'cause I knew shit was about to get real. I took a sip of my strawberry shake once Mariyah returned with the food, but my appetite had vanished.

Mariyah wasted no time diving in. She had already eaten two of her tenders before even looking up at me. "I'm sorry. It was so hectic today; I missed my lunch break," she admitted innocently.

"It's no need to explain, baby. Eat your food. That's why I bought it. Shit, eat mine too. Let me ask you this. Are there cameras in the rooms?"

"Yes, only the patients in ICU. Yes, Donk, Arianna was one of those patients. At the time we didn't know how serious her concussion was until we ran some tests."

My heart dropped to my dick when she dropped the unexpected jewels on me. Now the chances for me to take the rap for the body were very slim. I buried my head in the palm of my hands as I thought of the possibility of PJ going to prison.

"Look, Donk, I'm not green to none of this shit. I'm from the projects; I done seen it, heard it, and done it all. If you would've just gave me a heads up, I could've helped you dispose the trash." She whispered looking directly into my eyes.

"Shawty, it wasn't no plan, and I didn't kill no one. Me or my son." I admitted, standing to my feet.

"So that's it? You just going to bounce?" She asked, confused at the sudden change in my attitude.

"Yep," I responded, walking toward the door.

"Donk! Donk!" Mariyah called out, but I walked through the double doors and hopped into my whip.

Veins protruded from my forehead as I repeatedly smashed my fist against the steering wheel. I couldn't believe this shit was happening like that. Firs my baby girl, now PJ. I needed a drink and I needed something potent, and pronto. I couldn't deal with Persuasia and her attitude. I had to find someplace else. With no exact destination I swerved out the lot and quickly merged onto I-35.

Ring! Ring! I quickly picked up the phone after seeing the familiar number. "Yo!"

"Hey you!"

"Hey, baby. How are you, mama?"

"I'm okay. I um…I'm not that scared anymore, but I want to come home."

"I know, baby, and just know I'm doing everything I can."

"Well, Unc, I only got five minutes. We get a five-minute call once a week. It goes up to two if we're good."

"So, what you doing to do?"

"I'm going to be good so I can talk to you as much as I can. You think next time I can talk to Lil' Tim?"

"Of course, baby girl. Anything for you."

"Is PJ and Arianna okay?"

My chest tightened as I thought about PJ. I didn't want to mention anything just yet to sour her mood. I hoped like hell I wouldn't have to say anything at all. "They're okay. Arianna is home with us now."

"Kadejah, you have a minute left," someone in the background announced.

"Unc," she whispered.

"Huh? I'm here," I quickly responded.

"Aye, Um…Unc, I love you please tell PJ and them I love em' too," she spoke softly. I could hear the sadness in her voice. I imagined her crying silent tears.

"Mama, don't cry. You a big girl. You my big girl. Matter of fact, you a G. Just like Uncle Mun and Donk. G's don't cry. You'll be back out here with us soon. Steve will come see you soon. So will I, and whatever you do, tell Steve the truth."

"Okay, I will. I love you." She sighed.

"I love you too," I responded before I slowly removed the phone from my ear, allowing my eyes to linger on the screen. If my mother was alive today, she would be so disappointed in me right now. I pulled into the parking spot on the side of Buffalo Wild Wings. I figured a drink or two in my system would temporarily ease my disoriented mind.

"Hi, welcome to Buffalo Wild Wings. Table for one?" The host asked looking over my shoulder.

"Yeah, it's just me," I mumbled.

"Follow me," she stated leading the way.

The place wasn't shoulder-to-shoulder packed, but it was far from empty. "I don't need a table, I'm just going to chill at the bar," I decided, plopping down on the comfortable stool. I guess she didn't hear me as she continued on through. "A shot of Henny. Keep 'em coming," I requested to the chubby bartender. *I wish it would've been a female instead of a dude*, I thought.

"You got it," he lamely called out.

I turned my attention to the fifty-inch flat in front of me. The first round of the playoffs was soon to begin and I don't understand how I managed to completely forget. Boston Celtics and the Philadelphia Sixers. They were the first teams to play. I like the Boston Celtics. Kyrie my main guy. He'll put a nigga on his pockets with that crossover.

"I shouldn't even be here in this bullshit ass shack. You were supposed to have been here thirty minutes ago with my money, man!" The dude spoke in a loud tone.

I peered over in his direction. The frustration was quite dramatic. He repeatedly banged his forehead with the palm of his hand. I forced my eyes back on the screen. The game hadn't begun. It was only a few seconds before it started. "Come on, Boston!" I yelled feeling the two shots in my system.

"Oh, you for Boston, huh?" The frustrated white dude inquired.

"Hell, yeah. Philly can't fuck with us. They need more than Ben and the process," I quoted downing another shot.

"And Boston can beat Philly without Irving?" He asked knowingly.

"Hell yeah, nigga!" I assured placing the shot glass down on the counter forcefully.

"Want to bet?"

"Just give me a number. You ain't said shit."

"I got $1500. Philly beats Boston."

"I bet Boston with the whole series. You win, I pay you $1500. I win, you pay me $1500 and you can give me the $3500 once their series is over."

"Bet."

We shook hands, talked shit, and I cheered on the Celtics for the rest of the night. Just as I predicted, Boston won. I guess he assumed since Kyrie wasn't present that they couldn't hold their own.

"Kyle, and you?" He asked stepping to me.

"Donk," I replied.

He reached into his pocket, peeled off fifteen one hundred-dollar bills and placed it in my hand. "Dude, you toasted. Maybe you should let me give you a ride home or call someone to come get you." He suggested.

"Thanks, man, but I'll call my bitch." I slurred.

"Alright. Here's my number. Call me as soon the series done, or maybe before then so we can make a bet on tomorrow's game if you down."

"Portland and OKC. Hell yeah, you going to hear from me." I stated as I scrolled through my call history for Persuasia's number. "Aye. I, I'm at Buffalo Wild Wings on Thirty. Come and pick me up; I'm wasted," I told her through sips. I figured since I'm not the one driving I can keep getting toasted until she gets here.

"Okay, I'm on my way," she assured before hanging up.

Ah'Million

CHAPTER 10
PJ

Quite alarmed at my surroundings I took a deep breath and exhaled as I looked to my left at a fast-asleep Arianna. I almost forgot all about yesterday's mishaps until laid my eyes on the beautiful young lady who rested in my pajamas underneath my sheets. Although I didn't recall the blanket or removing my shoes. I slowly got up and folded the thin blanket before placing it on top of the chair, when I noticed Arianna's medicine on the dresser.

Maybe she already took them, I thought, eyeing the prescription on the bottle. I nudged her arm to awake her anyways. Arianna jumped up with a terrified expression on her face, not even realizing it was only me. She used the blanket to cover her face and as still as a bird she lay there motionless.

"Arianna? Aye, Arianna, it's me, PJ," I called out in a soft but welcoming tone. It was no need for her to be afraid anymore.

She quickly slid the covers down eyeing me suspiciously. A smile slowly spread across her face but not a single word escaped her lips.

I instantly thought about what the doctor had told cmy mom earlier. "You have to take your medicine so you can feel better." I attempted to convince her placing two of the orange, oversized pills in my hand. She sat up on her elbows as she patiently waited for me to retrieve a glass of water. I figured since I'm making my way around the house I would check and see if mama has already given Arianna her meds for the day. "Momma!" I yelled out as I headed to the kitchen. "Mo—" I froze up as I looked at the time on the oven. It was 11:49 p.m. "Damn, it's late," I mumbled, retrieving a bottle of water from the fridge.

I stood on the tip of my toes and grabbed a few snack size bags of Hot Cheetos and a box of oatmeal pies. On my way back to my room I peered out the blinds of the front window. I didn't see neither Donk nor my mother's car in the driveway. I found it kind of odd. If anyone would be out at this time it would be Donk. I didn't allow it to make me overthink or ponder, so I closed the blind and headed back into my room. Arianna was now leaned up against the headboard with her fingers intertwined. She shyly smiled once I entered then lowered her eyes back down to her fingers.

With a smile I rushed to her side, handing her the pills and cold water. "I brought snacks!" I quipped with excitement, holding the snacks in the air. She gave me one of those tight lip smiles and I lowered my hands, feeling dejected. I was hoping Arianna would be a bit enthused, but she wasn't.

I plopped down beside the bed after placing a few oatmeal pies and a bag of Hot Cheetos next to Arianna. I was about to stuff my face when I felt Arianna's cold hand on top of my forearm. I glanced up, sensing something was wrong when she slowly backed away on her knees. She pointed at the body part in between her legs and made a painful scowl. My words got caught in my throat as I looked at her dumbfounded. Tears welled up in her eyes as she softly patted the top of her "purse". I never knew the name of a woman's body part until one day my mother told Kadejah to tell her if someone touches her purse, which I later found out, women have two purses. I felt helpless the longer I gazed into Arianna eyes.

Fed up, I hopped out of the bed and was headed into the front room when I spotted the cream on the dresser. My reading was on a ninth-grade level, but it was words on the tube I couldn't understand. I was able to comprehend "Apply to the affected area twice a day." I walked slowly toward Arianna, feeling a bit hesitant. I figured I could wait for my mother, but I thought against it, not knowing her exact whereabouts. No telling what time she would return.

"Lay down, Arianna," I directed, fluffing the pillow before positioning her head on top of it. I slowly removed her bottoms as I looked into her painfilled eyes. Uneasiness crept over me, but I shook it off for the sake of my friend. As I inched Arianna's panties down, my mouth watered abruptly at the sight of her top. I inched them down further and the unpleasant sight made my heart fall to the pit of my stomach. I wasn't too familiar with how a woman's purse supposed to look, but I knew for certain it didn't supposed to look like Arianna's. The outer part was so swollen you could hardly see the slit that was usually down the middle. I assumed that was the *affected area*. I removed the lid from the tube and gently rubbed the cream across her lips.

Arianna closed her eyes during this process for a moment. She winced, but before long she was seductively squirming. Not knowing how to react, I secured the lid and pulled her panties up, followed by her bottoms. She opened her eyes, and to my surprise she wrapped her arms around my neck.

"It's okay, Arianna," I whispered, hugging her back, suddenly missing Kadejah at that very moment. I reached behind my head and grabbed Arianna forearms, removing them from around my neck. "It's okay now, Arianna. You got me and I'm not going anywhere." I promised, scanning her tear-stained face.

Without a response, just a nod of the head Arianna scooted back up to the headboard. I picked up the remote and powered on the TV. I loved sports but I know she probably wouldn't find basketball too enthusing, so I put it on Nickelodeon and we watched SpongeBob. A bag of hot Cheetos and two oatmeal pies later, Arianna was dozing off. My mother and Donk still hadn't returned.

BOOM! "FBI! We have a warrant for a Prichard Josey!"

My head snapped into the direction of a frightened Arianna. Without hesitation I swiftly dove underneath the bed. Sweat dripped down my forehead as I heard the countless footsteps rummaging through the house. Scared wasn't even the word as the warm liquid began to descend my pants leg. For a moment my breathing ceased.

Boom! Arianna shrieked loudly once the policemen barged in.

"Where's Prichard?" the officer yelled.

I could see nothing but their feet from underneath the bed. I only could imagine what was going on in Arianna's head.

"Check the closet!" the guy hollered. I closed my eyes, hoping one of us would just disappear, but that didn't happen. The flashlight forced me to open my eyes instantly. "Prichard, come out with our hands up!" The officer demanded. The huge gun almost made me shit myself.

I probably would've if the officer on the left didn't terrify me even more, which ceased the movement of my bowels. I rolled form underneath the bed and with lightning speed they were on my ass, cuffing me with a quickness. I looked over my shoulder at Arianna as they led me out of my room. Her face held no emotion as I mouthed the words *"I'm sorry."*

I sat inside a small room cuffed to a metal table. It was a bright light directly above the table I sat at; the room was empty, and I was waiting for someone, just anyone to walk through the big metal door. It felt like I'd been sitting on this hard ass chair for hours. Tears formed in my eyes as I thought about Kadejah and her situation, now me and mine. I would miss everyone, even Arianna if these white folks decided to stick this murder to me. Although it was an accident, I was the cause of his demise. *I wondered if momma and Donk at home and realized what has taken place.*

The light from the other side of the door made me squint as a tall white guy finally came into view. He wore an all-black t-shirt that had FBI on the center in white. He sat directly across from me with a manila envelope. "Hi, Prichard." He smiled, placing the envelope on the table. He was trying to act as if this was some type of friendly meeting, but I knew better. I nodded my head in response as I focused my gaze on the envelops. "Prichard, look. You tell me what I need to know, and I'll personally take you back home myself." He stated staring a hole in my head. His pale blue eyes were enchanting but yielding at the same time.

His words were music to my ears as I looked up at him with hope. Kadejah had always told me the police were the bad guys, but in this situation I felt like he was my super hero. In one breath I informed the officer of everything that took place inside Arianna's room.

"He was raping your friend?" He inquired, lifting his right brow.

"Yes, sir," I answered proudly. Assuming my crime would be justified due to his wrongdoing.

"Prichard Josey, you have the right to remain silent. Anything you say can be and will be used against you."

I looked at the officer. His mouth continued to move but I couldn't hear, let alone comprehend, anything he was saying as I zoned out into what felt like another world. Two more officers came into the room and escorted me out and down the hall. In utter shock I was nearly being dragged. For some odd reason I couldn't get my feet and my mental on one accord. It was as if I was standing in quicksand. Now I see why Kadejah called them bad guys.

Ah'Million

CHAPTER 11
LIL' TIM

Beep! Bando was at the table counting up the loot while I was on the sofa busting down the bricks. The spot was doing numbers; just this one alone. Not including the duck off out in Tyler or the one on the other side of the tracks. Every man had a small team built around them. It was just up to them to make sure everything was a good amongst the members. Reggie was so about his money and into his occupation he only kept one worker at his spot. Morning, noon, and night he was posted. He hardly went to the club unless it was an event for the squad. Other than that, he was making money. Dude had trust issues, but his skills to decipher the fake was on point, nonetheless.

"Aye, how long you gon' be over here, fam?" Bando called out as he held the phone away from his ear.

"About thirty more minutes and then I'm going to head out to check on Lil' Reggie," I responded. He said something into the phone, but I couldn't make out his words before my phone chimed in. It was Peaches. "Wadup doe?" I answered coolly.

"Oh, you big kicking it, huh? What time you going to pull up on me?" She questioned with a hint of attitude.

I chuckled at her assumption. She knew not to speak too much on anything. "Give me an hour to two. I still got a couple moves to make." I responded truthfully.

"Okay, daddy. What you want to eat?" She asked seductively.

"Pussy," I shot back.

"Tim! Foreal!" She chuckled.

"Whatever you cook. Just nothing red."

"Nothing red?" she challenged.

"Yeah, nothing red! Spaghetti, meatloaf, lasagna…nothing red," I explained.

"Okay, Tim." She sighed before ending the call.

Mun told me years ago, "When you balling and fuckin' wit' these hoes, don't trust them with nothing. They'll try to trap you in more than one way."

My auntie Verna from the Nola, she beyond superstitious, but I always took heed to the things she told me. And eating everyone's cooking was definetly a no-no. All in all, none of it made sense until I realized just how cut-throat a hoe can be.

I was kicking it with a chick from the 'burbs. Boojie bitches just as cut-throat as the ratchet ones. She pulled up to the spot. I didn't have no more rubbers, so I told her to stop and get a box. She said she was already prepared. So, I'm like, "Cool". Well, she pulled up looking good enough to eat. As soon as she stepped through the door, I'm ready. She get fully naked before I even undress. My mans so hard he almost tore through my briefs. She retrieves the condom from her purse, use her teeth to rip it open. I remove my briefs and allow her to do the honors of sliding the rubber on.

"Bust it open," I demand while I slowly stroked my manhood.

"Come get it," she begged, but I wanted to enjoy the view before diving in.

Shortly a shot of pre-cum oozed out, and to my surprise it dripped on to the palm of her hand. Completely stunned, I say.

"What the fuck? Let me see that wrapper," I demanded, snatching it out of her trembling hands. I could see the fear in her eyes. The condom wrapper was full of tiny holes, some bigger than the others, but they were all noticeable like she had taken a sewing needle and poked until her arms got tired. I kicked her in the side and slapped her across the face with my hand that was covered in pre-cum. I put her out but kept her purse and her clothes. Pussy and titties swinging, I didn't give a damn. So, yeah, ever since then I been super cautious.

"Aye, fam, what you got going for tomorrow?" Bando inquired as he sat down next to me on the sofa.

"I'm going to see Kadejah and hook up with Donk. Why? What's up?" I responded.

"You know around the playoff season the strip club be lit. I wanted to know if you'll fall through with me," he stated putting fire to the Kush blunt.

"Yeah, I'll slide through with you for a few hours," I agreed as we dapped and put the blunt in rotation. I hurried off to the restroom to piss before heading out. Once I was done, I noticed a black, silk like material clung onto the tip of my shoes. "The fuck?" I mumbled, pulling it off, shaking my head at the underwear. "Bitches leaving they draws and shit!" I yelled, tossing the panties on Bando's head.

Oddly he took longer than what I would have to remove them. "Nigga, you heard *Middle Child* by J. Cole?" Bando asked me in between puffs.

"I don't think so. Play it." I was curious about J. Cole's new hit. Dude was truly a lyricist. The beat dropped and I found myself lost in the lyrics. The beat really complimented the song, and before I knew it, I was bobbing my head and doing the bop. I couldn't jig but I could bop like the niggas in Florida. By the time the song ended I was turned up. Dude had bars for days; he just went the fuck off.

"He was on that hoe, huh?" Bando asked with a cocky smile.

"Hell yeah. I'm 'bout to go play that bitch right now!" I said standing to my feet. I grabbed the dope and the cash before heading toward the door.

"Nigga, that wasn't thirty minutes, but I'll link up with you tomorrow. Be safe, boy," Bando commented, opening the front door.

"Nigga, who that?" I asked, pointing toward the car that pulled up to the spot.

With a devilish grin, Bando said, "Some bad bitches. I guess since you about to go, it's more fun for me."

"You tried to set some shit up without telling me. You gone get enough of playing with these hoes in this spot. Hold it down. I love you," I preached, walking down the steps and out the gate. Something about the chick on the passenger side was a bit too familiar, but I glanced and kept it pushing. *Ring! Ring!* I looked down at the screen that displayed a picture of me and Donk. "Talk to me," I answered quickly.

"Aye, take twenty grand to ol' boy grandmother house and slide it in the mailbox." Donk ordered.

"Bet," I stated before ending the call.

Twenty minutes later I parked across the street from the spot after dropping the cash off at Meech's grandmother's house. I could only imagine how Mariyah felt. I didn't see her often 'cause Meech did his best to hide her, but I saw her enough to remember her face and name. However, that was years ago. Music blared onto the street from a house two doors down that had their front door wide open. I didn't know which side was more hood: the East or West. I'm not going to lie; the West was a bit more lit than the East, and the fiends came by the dozen on this side.

"'Bout time, nigga," Reggie capped, opening the door as we embraced each other with a handshake.

"What's up Tim?" Ceelo called out, pausing the video game.

"What up boy?" I shot back tossing the dope on the table. Ceelo was one of the workers Reggie picked. He was a chubby mixed cat, but he was all about his cash. He wasn't a sloppy, fat nigga. He had swag and kept his hygiene up.

"Bag that shit up, C. We almost out of that other shit," Reggie directed, throwing the duffel bag to Ceelo. Reggie was a smooth cat. No kids, no bitch and I don't think he was going to change that anytime soon. You know how ESPN commentators label Kevin Durant as a gym rat 'cause he in the gym 24-7? That's Reggie. He just do his in the spot. I have to tell the nigga when he needed to go get faded and he'll call his mobile barber. He don't give a damn 'bout nothing but the bag. He was literally the type who wouldn't get any play if he was being judged on his outer appearance. I can say when it was time to pop out, he fixed up damn good.

"Aye, nigga, me and Bando hitting the club up tomorrow, you coming?" I asked thumbing through the hundred-dollar bills.

"Nah, I don't want to miss out on a dollar, fam." He responded rubbing his fresh bald fade.

"Come on man, you already got you a fresh fade; fuck with ya boy!" I joked.

"Alright, man…two hours, that's it," he agreed with a smile.

"Oh, yeah…I'm bouncing after two hours, too. That's Bando ass want to spend a night at the club and shit," I commented, slapping hands with Reggie. "I'm going to hit Chris and see if he want to slide through," I decided, pulling out my Samsung Galaxy.

"Nah, fam. I'm not too fond of big boy," Reggie responded, rubbing his goatee with a hint of uneasiness in his eyes.

"Man, Chris a real one, no doubt about it," I assured, dismissing his feelings.

"I mean, I ain't saying I don't like him 'cause I don't know dude, but it's something. I just can't pinpoint it. I could be tripping though 'cause usually I'm able to hit it on the money. It's something, maybe it's petty, but it's something." He explained with squinted eyes.

"I don't know. I'm not no fool either, but I've never peeped a crumb of disloyalty." I responded confidently using my thumb and index finger to demonstrate the size of a crumb.

"Well, there you go, fam." He agreed dropping the subject. A few fiends knocked while Reggie and I chopped it up about some major moves that were about to be put in play. I had to silence my phone 'cause Peaches wouldn't stop hitting me up.

"Alright, y'all. I'm about to get out of here. Be easy." I walked toward the door.

"Alright, Tim." Ceelo called out.

Reggie walked with me to the door where we shook hands and I proceeded to exit.

I walked into Peaches 2-bedroom condo on Parklane, removed my shoes at the door and plopped down on the sofa. "Peaches!" I yelled out, picking up the remote from the table. I flipped through the channels and placed the remote back once I landed on the ESPN commentator discussing Kyrie's injury.

Peaches came from the kitchen with a plate in her hand. She wore a spaghetti strap shirt, booty shorts, her skin was golden like a Hostess Twinkie, she even had this glow. I could tell the bitch had an attitude. She placed the plate in front of me then turned on her heels, headed for the kitchen.

"Peaches, come sit yo' ass down on the sofa."

Her hair was in a low ponytail with the part down the middle. The long hair enhanced her sex appeal. She sat next to me with her arms folded across her chest.

"Oh, so you not eating?" I asked looking in her direction while she was motionless, feeling sulky.

"I lost my appetite, Tim," she responded, rolling her eyes. I grew exceptionally quiet and I assumed that must've drove Peaches nuts. "Tim, why don't you trust me, man?" She asked disturbed. The shrimp fettuccini, lemon peppered steak and garlic bread really hit the spot, but I was not in the mood to argue with her ass. "I'm just saying, Lil' Tim, you don't trust me after all this time?" She continued, hopping up from the couch, hovering over me. I sucked my teeth and placed my feet on the table, paying her absolutely no mind. I'm not going to lie, the fragrance she had on lingered around my nostrils. Before long I was undressing her with my eyes. "Tim!" she called out.

"Peaches, shut the fuck up," I stated calmly as I watched ESPN through squinted eyes. She smacked her lips and moved in front of the TV screen. "You doing all this for what? Dang. Huh? If this dick is what you want, here, take it, it's yours," I insisted, removing my feet from the table and spreading my legs apart, further than usual.

With a devious grin on her face, she slowly dropped to her knees. I know she was about to put it down when she wrapped her ponytail into a bun, making herself comfortable, shifting from her knees to her butt as she sat at my lap with her legs crossed. She looked up at me with lust filled eyes while unzipping my pants, then slowly removing my jeans and briefs in one swift motion. She took turns raising my legs as she removed my pants one leg at a time. I scooted to the edge of the sofa and grabbed another pillow from the other end of the couch to comfortably position myself. Like a singer with a mic, she went on stage, wrapping her luscious lips around the head of my mans. She secured the top of my dick in between the roof of her mouth and the top of her tongue, using her saliva and the motion of her tongue to slide it in and out with ease.

"Don't start with that teasing shit," I commented, biting down on my bottom lip. Like a savage she attacked my pole with her tongue, dragging it from the base to the tip. She repeated the move and in one swift motion my nine-inch, brick hard dick was down her throat. "Damn, girl" I whispered as my eyes began to roll to the back of my head.

"Mmmmmhmmm, hmmm," she moaned with confidence.

I grabbed a hold of her bun and quickly pumped my mans in and out of her mouth. I was ready to bust, she was playing games. She broke free from my grip, blowing a kiss in my direction. "Come on, what you doing?" I asked impatiently, eyes nearly popping out the sockets. I hated when she played like that.

"Shut up," she demanded, getting back to it like it was nothing to it. She tucked her lips to cover her teeth and sucked and slurped me dry. Moans and grunts escaped my mouth as my toes began to curl. I was so caught up in the moment I couldn't even utter a word. Before I knew it, my semen shot down her throat. She swallowed my shit as if it tasted like Dasani, then used the back of her hand to wipe whatever was left away.

"Sit on my lap," I demanded, leaning back on the sofa.

Peaches stood to her feet and removed her clothes before climbing on top. "I love you, Tim," she claimed as she positioned herself on the tips of her toes. It's like my dick had senses and he could smell the pussy that lingered over him. He instantly sprang upward and Peaches slid down the pole slowly. Only taking half of the dick, she eased back up and rolled around on the tip. I grabbed her by her slim waist and pulled her down, forcing her to take all 9 inches. "Ooohhh, Tim, why you... Why you do that?" she moaned in between breaths, biting down on her lip while gazing into my eyes.

"Who pussy is this?" I asked looking into her eyes while spreading her butt cheeks further apart as I sped up my pace.

"This-This...is your pussy, Tim. Oohhh, baby, it's yours. I promise!" she yelled in pure ecstasy. "I'm coming!" She cried breathlessly, pushing away the loose strands that were stuck to her face. Her body stiffened as she wrapped her arms around my neck. "This my dick, Tim," she spoke between clenched teeth in the midst of her climax. I was just seconds away. I tightly gripped her thighs as I shot my load inside of her. Drained Peaches slowly stood to her feet. "Come on, daddy." She pouted, taking a hold of my hand and leading the way to the bedroom where we passed out.

CHAPTER 12
KADEJAH

Hearing Uncle Donk's voice really soothed my little soul. Ms. Smith asked me twenty-one questions regarding my past and current life before I was able to go to bed. As soon as the metal door shut behind me reality sank in. Surprisingly I noticed Tru was on the bottom bunk fast asleep. I rather her to have been my roommate than Kedra or Shun. They were a bit too nosey for my liking. I tried to think of it as if they were afraid for me. I tried not to make too much noise as I stepped onto the stool and climbed on top of the bunk. The mattress was hard as cardboard. *So much for a pillow*, I thought, rolling up and fluffing the sides of the sheet to my liking, although it was nothing like my pillow at home. It would do for the time being.

I turned on my side and let the tears cascade onto my hand-made pillow. I cupped my hand around my nose every time I sniffled, trying my best not to awake Tru. I knew it didn't once I felt her finger poke me in my back.

"Kadejah," she called out. I turned around and met her gaze. Her eyes were desirous and hypnotizing. "You alright?" she asked, rubbing the sleep from her eyes.

Quickly using the back of my hand, I wiped the tears from my face. "Yeah, I'm good," I lied.

Tru sat on the stool that was connected to the table, lifting her shirt before sitting down revealing her boxers.

"They have those here?" I pointed.

"No, my homeboy gave me these. They're housed underneath us. They go to court with us and hand out our trays sometimes." She explained. "Aye, Shun, she cool and all but she's a liar. Downplaying the situation so you won't be scared when really your shit is as serious as it looks," she confirmed, rubbing her fingers through her braids. Although Tru was speaking the truth, her words brought tears to my eyes, and before long they were pouring down "Man, Kadejah, stop crying." She stated, climbing on top of the stool. Balancing on the stool she leaned forward onto my bed where we were face to face. "Stop crying, mama, I just didn't want you believing any and everything. Trust me, I know how this shit works." She assured, stroking my hair. We were a bit closer than normal and I could smell Tru's breath. Surprisingly, it had no smell whatsoever.

"Okay," was all I could say, as I lay there motionless with a tear-stained face looking up into Tru beautiful eyes. The stare down felt like hours, but it was barely a minute. An eerie feeling came over me and I wanted to react, but I didn't know exactly how to react.

"Goodnight. Kadejah," she stated, jumping off the stool.

"Goodnight, Tru," I shot back.

I awoke the next morning with drool on my pillow. My side was aching, and my nose was stuffy.

Tru was awoke and staring out of the metal mesh on the door that faced the day room. "You want some?" She turned on her heels with a beef Ramen noodle in one hand and a white plastic spoon in the other.

"No," I shot back with a look of disgust. I hope I didn't offend her, but I didn't feel comfortable eating off no one's spoon.

"Okay," she retorted. She shrugged her shoulders while pacing the floor. Me and Tru talked and laughed for quite some time; she was hilarious. She mimicked different characters from movies and told me stories about herself and friends before being incarcerated. I was clinching my stomach laughing, watching her jig like she was at a club. "Me and my potnas went to this teen club and this song came on. We wasn't in the club two minutes and he was dropping it low, jigging through the door," she joked, demonstrating her friend's move.

"Kadejah Richards, get dressed. You have a visit!" Ms. Smith announced.

I jumped off the bed and grabbed my hygiene bag off the table.

"Who do you think coming to see you?" Tru asked before plopping down on her bed.

"My Uncle Donk," I responded enthused. I grabbed my comb out the bag and combed my hair forward into a high bun. Tru put my toothpaste on my toothbrush while I combed my hair. "I'm ready!" I yelled while brushing my teeth. I rinsed and used the back of my hand to wipe the rest of any remains.

Ms. Smith walked me out to the vestibule where I waited for a few seconds.

A tall, dark-skinned guy rounded the corner. "I got her, Ms. Smith. Come this way," he said, as he waited at the end of the hallway.

The walk was quick yet interesting to the visitation area. Once I walked into the room, it was about ten other juveniles lined up against the wall. It was a two-way window on the other side and the visitors were huddled up looking for their children. I didn't see Donk or anyone else familiar.

"Each one of y'all stand next to an empty room one at a time." The male officer directed.

I let the other kids rush to an empty room and I fell back patiently. After seeing everyone posted I quickly walked to one of the empty rooms at the end of the hall.

"Right this way," a different male officer directed, leading the crowd of visitors.

Relatives start swarming in and I immediately scanned the crowd. Feeling confused as the wrinkles formed across my forehead, I peered closer looking for my family. The male officer was closing the doors on the family members that were seated inside the rooms, when I spotted Uncle Donk and Lil' Tim walk through the door. I ran up to them, wrapping my arms around both of them at the same time. I was ecstatic, but I could see the depression written all over their faces. "Come on, y'all," I called out over my shoulder, leading them to my visitation room.

The officer closed the door once we were seated. He stared at Lil' Tim and Uncle Donk a little longer than usual, but once they gave him the look of death he retreated to his duty post.

"Hey, baby girl," he greeted suddenly, reaching across the table to caress my hands.

"Heeeyyy, Unc." I cheerfully responded.

Lil' Tim jut peered at me with disbelief. Looking into his narrowed slits instantly made me feel remorseful for my actions. I lowered my head in guilt. "Kadejah, I'm not mad at you, mama," Lil' Tim spoke up. You just don't deserve to be in a place like this for defending yourself and loved ones. You truly did what you had to and was supposed to do. I'm upset with myself for not being there to do that for you." Lil' Tim expressed sincerely. He looked as if he wanted to cry.

"It's okay, I'm just ready to come home. Is there any good news from Steve?" I inquired.

"He's filing a motion of discovery which is basically to see what evidence they have against you. The good thing is the store had cameras on the inside and the outside, and if it went down like you say it did, you'll be out in no time." Uncle Donk explained.

I knew how it all happened and I didn't take away nor did I add to the story. We spent the rest of our time joking and laughing. Something was a little off about Uncle Donk, but I decided not to pry.

"One minute left to say your goodbyes and wrap it up!" The male officer yelled. I slowly stood to my feet, not wanting the visit to come to an end. The back of my eyes began to burn as tears welled inside me.

"Don't do it! Big girls don't cry, and don't be discussing your case with none of them little knuckle heads," Lil' Tim whispered, wrapping his strong arms around me.

I immediately blinked the tears away. His cologne invaded my nostrils and I hugged him tightly. Honestly, I didn't want to turn him lose so I pretended to sob to buy myself a little more time in his embrace. "I love you, Lil' Tim," I whined in between sniffles. His torso felt like a brick wall and his cologne was mesmerizing.

"Times up," the CO shouted, causing me to jump. I backed away from Lil' Tim. I hadn't even hugged my Uncle Donk yet.

Uncle Donk snatched me into a tight hug then placed a soft peck on my cheek. "I love you, baby girl. I'll be back soon. In the meantime, hit me up whenever you can." He stated before walking in the opposite direction.

I lined up against the wall with everyone else as we watched our families leave. Lil' Tim looked over his shoulder at me once he made it out the door. Instinctively I lowered my head.

Everyone was seated in the day room once I returned from my visit. The seat across from Tru was empty again. I'm wondering this time if she purposely made it available. I spotted Kedra and Shun sitting behind her, clowning early.

"So who came an—" Tru attempted to ask.

"Who was that? What they say?" Shun chimed in. I looked from Tru to Shun confused as who to answer first. Tru waved her hand in the air excusing herself while rolling her eyes. Shun shot Tru a dumbfounded look, but she knew exactly what just occurred.

"It was my uncle and my friend Lil' Tim," I said cheerfully, plopping down on the chair.

"So, did they say anything about your case?" Shun asked.

"Yeah, the lawyer is filing motions right now, but things are looking good." I admitted. I wish I felt as confident as I sounded. Tru still held a look of irritation. Despite what she thought of Shun, I acutally liked her. I hadn't witnessed her other side. Not yet anyways.

"Tru!" Shun called. "Man, I didn't mean to barge in. I was just as excited as you was."

"Yeah. Tru. Yo red ass always getting mad about something. Cheer up, nigga," Kedra spoke up.

Tru attempted to hide her smile but couldn't. "Shut up, Kedra, I ain't mad," Tru shot back, sitting up in her seat. "Aye, Kadejah, you like girls?" Tru asked randomly. From the look in her eyes I could tell the question wasn't so random. Maybe she had it on her mind for some time now.

"Hell no!" I shouted, loathing the thought of such interaction. I've never been with a female nor did the thought ever cross my mind.

Immediately I recanted my kindergarten days as I thought of Angel. I had just graduated Headstart. This particular year was my

2nd year of elementary. I was a few days late starting school due to some sort of documents that needed to be verified. That's what Mama Bre told me. By this time everyone had their group— or should I say clique, friend or best friend. Angel was a mix breed with curly hair. Her eyes were small and slanted like the people from China, she had a small gap in between her two front teeth, but overall, she was beautiful. Although Angel had her three friends, she hung around every day she was drawn to me. She would bring my favorite snack to school which was Fruit Roll-ups and gushes.

She didn't try prying into my past life like most. Instead we talked a lot about the future. One day during restroom break, me and Angel were waiting in line. Our teacher directed the restroom break, two students at a time. Ms. Johnson would just yell, "Next!" from her desk. She didn't have to be right there for us to do the right thing, everyone knew not to play with Ms. Johnson's ability.

"It always smell so good on—" I began to praise, but my words were cut off by Angel's lips being pressed against mine. She shoved me inside the stall and locked it behind us.

Caught by surprise, I threw my hands up in an attempt to pro-test, but honestly, I wanted to experience what she had in mind, although the expression on my face said otherwise.

She forced me down onto the toilet seat and straddled my lap. Next, she took my hands and placed them on her backside then cupped my face with the palms of her hands before kissing me aggressively, while moaning softly. Our little secret felt like it went on forever, but it really only lasted five minutes. Afterwards, we didn't discuss what happened, but we knew what to expect every day, at the same time. Sometimes I was the aggressor, forcefully shoving my tongue down her throat, although I didn't really know what I was doing. My hands roamed her body, as I instinctively felt her feminine parts.

Our little rendezvous went on until the end of the school year. I was hoping we would pick back up the next school year, but I never saw her again. Still to this day, that's a secret I've never shared and don't plan on sharing.

"My bad, I didn't mean to offend you," Tru apologized, throwing her hands up in supplication.

After reminiscing about Angel, I instantly felt a tinge of guilt. I hadn't thought about being with a girl but I had enjoyed Angel and our secret affair.

DONK

Stressed wasn't the word. I couldn't think, let alone sleep knowing my babies were in trouble. Me and Hennessey have always had a relationship, but since Kadejah vanished, me and the potent liquor had become best friends. I know the drunkenness was causing mental and emotional detachment which was killing Persuasia. But I honestly didn't know any other way to deal. I never been in love. Hell, this is the first time I've been in a real relationship. I hated seeing bae moping around, and not being her usual jolly self, but I couldn't bring myself to utter a word. I felt at ease not saying anything. I wanted to console her 'cause I know she missed PJ like a muthafucka. I've recanted that moment in my head a hundred times, and if I was little PJ I would've done the same thing. Proud of his courageous act, I allowed my mind to drift off to a time I wasn't so courageous when I should've done exactly what PJ did.

"Get in here, Mun!" My mother yelled. The three of us shared a bedroom in the 2-bedroom, 2-bathroom duplex located in Pleasant Grove.

I stood, Quaylo sat Indian style on the floor, and Mun leaned on the railing of the bunkbed, occupying the barely furnished space, fearfully anticipating the beating Mun was promised. That day my mother had discovered the report card he claimed to have never received, which was issued to us a month ago.

"Don't make me call you again!" she hollered.

My heart was beating rapidly. I slightly pinched my armpit to relieve the sudden itch. Mun dragged himself out of our room and into my mother's, giving us one last look over his shoulder.

Whap! The belt sounded off against Mun's flesh as his cry pierced the air. Whap! He yelled at the top of his lungs. We came to the conclusion that if we do a lot of hollering and crying it'll shorten the ass whooping, but I guess the method doesn't always work.

"Put your hands on the bed." My mother's boyfriend demanded. You would've thought a tape recorder was on repeat as many times as we heard him say that.

Whap! The beating continued. Me and Quaylo looked at one another, flinching every time the belt connected with Mun's flesh, Teror-stricken and tear-stained faces. I was trying to hold up enough courage to walk in. It continued for what felt like hours.

Finally I heard my mother's boyfriend say, "Pull up your pants and go to your room."

Me and Quaylo wiped our faces and opened the door to let Mun in. His chest heaved, his teeth chattered, and his eyes were red and puffy as he used the wall to balance himself. Me and Quay noticed him struggling and guided him to the bed.

"Sit down, Mun," I stated while he squatted several times in an attempt to sit on the bottom bunk.

"I can't," he mumbled.

"Okay, lay on your stomach," said Quaylo. She helped him to his knees.

I stood off to the side, in disbelief, monitoring Mun's slow and feeble movements. I knew it had to be bad if he couldn't move because Mun was tough. But I had no idea just how bad it was until I saw the thick welts all over his backside.

"Look at how swollen they are." Quaylo's voice cracked as she looked up at me and pointed to the horrible welts across Mun's bottom.

My eyes teared up and I dropped my head in defeat. Although I was only eight years old, I felt like a punk for not helping him. Even though it would've led to me getting my was whooped too, I felt I should've came to his defense. I told myself I would never let that shit happen to him again.

There was no doubt Kadejah sensed there was something wrong. I'm just relieved she didn't probe. To know that PJ was just a few feet below her in one of those same cells was disheartening. Steve explained that there was no way I could take the charge for PJ because everything was recorded on camera.

The camera wasn't exactly a curse in this situation because, at least, it showed that Arianna was truly being sexually assaulted. The judge could see the evidence on tape and decide to show mercy on PJ.

Seeing the tears in PJ's eyes earlier disturbed my soul. The older boys in there had been telling him that he'd get a sentence of life in prison. Persuasia couldn't make it to that visit, but she promised to make the next one. How did he feel about that? I wondered.

A text came to my phone from Kyle.

Me: What's up

Kyle: I got 2 bets

Me: What's that

We texted back and forth until a call came in, interrupting me.

"Hello?" I answered.

"Donk, I hope you're doing better. Come bless me with your presence so I can ease some tension." It sounded like the chick from the hospital.

"Mya?" I sought confirmation.

"Yes," she confirmed.

"Okay, text me the address."

***

An hour later, I was pulling up to Mya's house, which was surprisingly located in the hood. When I got inside, I was pleasantly surprised to see that the interior was much better than the outside. She led me to a seat in the living room, and then she retreated to the kitchen for a few minutes.

"Okay, you can come in here and sit at the table," she announced. "I hope you're hungry because I cooked for you."

I smiled and went to take a seat at the kitchen table. Delicious aromas caressed my nose. A minute later, I watched her as she walked toward me with a plate on her hand.

Mya sat the plate down in front of me while she went to retrieve hers. "Damn, what's this, ma? This shit smell good!" I stated eyeing the contents on my plate.

"This pepperoni and spinach calzones with orange beef and broccoli with rice." She stated. The shit smelled delicious and I didn't hesitate diving in. "You want more?" Mya smirked sitting beside me.

"Nah, mama, I'm good," I responded, sitting my plate on the table and picking up the bottle of Hennessey, pouring myself a drink.

"I'm sorry. It's a coke on top of the fridge and it's a cold one inside." She apologized.

"Oh, I drink it straight, but can you grab me a cup of ice?" I asked picking up my plate off the table and finishing my food. I looked at Mya's pictures that decorated her shelves while waiting on the ice. "Aye, Mya," I called out.

"Yes?" She stood behind me so close I could feel her breast on my back.

"Why you got that vase so high up? It looks so out of place," I inquired. Honestly it looked like it would've fell if a nigga came through thumpin'.

"Those are my sister ashes," she replied.

I turned around and instantly saw the pain in her tight eyes. "I'm sorry," I apologized cupping her cheek with my left hand.

"It's okay, I'm better now a days," she assured backpedaling. She sat my ice down and continued to eat her meal.

"So, what's up?" I asked before taking a seat next to her.

"If I can, and if you need me to, I'll testify," she stated in between bites.

"What can you say to help?" I asked puzzled.

"I don't know; whatever. I'll lie if need be, Donk," she admitted.

I was taken aback by her response. "So, you'll get on the stand and lie?" I asked not believing shorty. "Why you want to help me?" I added.

"I just do. Most importantly, I want to help your junior, especially since her dad took advantage of her the way he did. Our staff— well let me say *their* staff since I was fired yesterday— should have been monitoring those cameras and your son wouldn't be where he is." She explained sincerely. One thing I loved more than a bad bitch was a loyal bitch.

"Okay, so you don't have a job?" I inquired.

"Yeah, I work at Methodist Hospital," she responded.

"Which one? Do you need anything?"

"The one in Oak Cliff, and no, I'm fine."

Damn, I got to play shit safe. She work at the same hospital Persuasia works at. I knew she would be on her "I'm good" shit, but I had something for that. "Mya," I spoke in a hushed tone, turning my head in her direction.

"Yes?" she answered.

"I'm going to get going. This *Hen* got a nigga ready to sin. If I stay for another minute I'm going to end up knocking you off and that vase might hit the flo'."

Mya burst out laughing at my comment. She was goofy as hell. I enjoyed the vibe. She smacked her lips before parting them. "For real, Donk, you going to just burn out on me?"

"Look, Mya, I got a ol' lady and she don't like the idea of me passing her dick out. For the first time in my life I'm trying to do right," I admitted, standing to my feet.

"Okay, I feel you. I knew you were taken the first day I saw you. Dudes like you aren't single anymore," Mya stated with her legs crossed. The green spaghetti strapped shirt hugged her breast, exposing her rock-hard nipple prints. The gray booty shorts only made it complicated for me to walk out the door. Her long and thick legs were smooth and flawless, and the floral artwork on her thighs were impeccable. "Let me at least pour you a drink for the road," she suggested, pouring the Henny on the ice. Before passing me the glass she stuck her hand deep down in her crotch, rotated her fingers before slowly pulling her glossy fingers out. She used her finger to stir the Henny in a circular motion. I scrunched my face at her boldness. She slurped the Henny and whatever else off her fingers before blowing me a kiss.

I took a sip of my drink while giving her eye contact. "I don't mind the extra flavor in my drink. As long as it's no hair in my food, I'm good." I winked, grabbing the doorknob.

"Oh, never that," she confirmed. In one swift motion she tugged at her shorts exposing her shaved pussy.

The sight of it made me forget where I was going to begin with. I turned to the door, yanking it open before I changed my mind. The fresh breeze outdoors was like a blunt to a nigga in rehab. The young niggas who was posted up at first were no longer in sight. I slowly descended the steps. The .45 had my pants hanging off my ass. I lifted my jeans by the crotch and swaggered to my truck. I quickly got Steve on the line.

"What's up, Donk?" Steve answered all proper and shit.

"Aye, one of the staff at the hospital said she would testify on PJ's behalf," I informed, backing out of the parking space.

"And say what?" Steve asked dumbfounded.

"Whatever you need her to say. Lies and all," I stated proudly.

"Oh okay, I just might have something," he mentioned.

"Okay, keep me posted," I stated.

"You betcha," Steve retorted, ending the call.

"You watching the Crawford Fight tonight?" I peered at the text from Kyle. *This white boy just don't get enough,* I thought.

"No, I wasn't, but how much you talking?" I replied.

"I got 15,000 Crawford loses," he stated.

"Oh, that's a bet. Where you at?"

"Same as yesterday." Kyle was really starting to talk my lingo. If it's money in the mix, I'm in the midst. I shot a text to Lil' Tim as I made my way to the crowded sports bar— a lot of people with a lot of noise, entertainment and money to keep my mind off reality.

Me: *Meet me at the buffalo wild wings off 30 when you get the chance.*

Tim: *Bet. I'm going to swing through soon as I leave the club.*

I put my phone inside the empty cup holder and peeled off as I turned up the volume.

Ah'Million

CHAPTER 13
LIL' TIM

"Pack in the mail, it's gone. She like how I smell; cologne. I just signed a deal; I'm on. Yeah, yeah." DaBaby's latest hit *Suge* blasted through the club. A thick yella chick on stage made her ass cheeks jump to the beat. The place was lit, no lie. Me, Reggie, and Chris sat in VIP. Chris was back and forth being Chris, trying to bag more hoes. That dude was something else with that pimp shit. Reggie sat in the middle of the leather sectional slouched, one hand nursing his glass of Crown and the other one rested on his Glock. That boy stayed ready. Bando, on the other hand, was wilding but he knew he could wild out 'cause he had a click of real niggas that wouldn't miss a beat. Two bad bitches entertained Bando.

A neck full of ice and a bottle in hand, he poured the expensive champagne down the crack of the stripper's ass while positioned on the floor on all fours as she did the right cheek, left cheek. He pulled a hundred dollar bill out of his pocket and tossed it toward the other stripper. "Lick it up." He demanded through arrogant eyes while reclining on the sectional.

Like a thirsty dog, the gorgeous butter pecan complexioned stripper planted kisses on the other stripper's ass cheeks. She positioned herself directly behind her; her ass was directly in front of her face. She placed her succulent lips at the bottom of her pear shaped ass and used her hands to spread her butt cheeks apart, abruptly slurping whatever champagne that rested in the crevice. I looked on at the tempting and seductive yet degrading scene. Bando was hypnotized. His worst enemy could've walked up and he wouldn't have even noticed. Amigos' hit *Pure Water* faded into the speakers. A slim thick chocolate chick caught my attention.

"Aye, come here, girl!" I yelled to the chick that was headed for the stage.

She turned around and walked my way but was stopped in mid-stride by a big nigga who seemed a bit too drunk. His face was all too familiar. He whispered something in the chick's ear and she started smiling

Just as I was about to turn my head, something in my mind clicked, and through narrow slits slowly rose to my feet. "That's that damn, Dino," I mumbled.

"What's up, Lil' Tim?" Reggie asked as he sat up straight, sitting the half empty glass on the table.

"I'm about to go get at this bitch ass nigga." I stated, keeping a keen eye on Dino and the stripper.

"Who?" Reggie asked with squinted eyes, hand still on Glock.

"That nigga right there talking to that lil' thick black bitch." I pointed. "When I was in the A some years ago, him and his entourage jumped me, and if it wasn't for Bando, I would've been dead or a vegetable. That's how I met Bando. I didn't even know the nigga and he helped me," I explained.

I guess Bando must have heard his name. When he finally looked up he saw Reggie and me standing. I really thought Dino was one of the few Bando actually hit. The part that perturbs me the most is, *why the fuck is he in my city? Who invited this nigga? Where he come from?* I thought.

Without hesitation I headed toward Dino. Reggie followed suit. I could hear Bando calling my name, but I didn't slow my pace. "Say, bitch ass nigga, I been looking for you, boy," I stated with my hand pointed in his face.

"Nigga, if it's 'bout this bitch you can have her." Dino responded holding his hands up in surrender.

"Oh, you know what it's 'bout and this bitch ain't it." I smiled, exposing the diamonds that rested on all thirty-two of my teeth.

Dino removed his shades and his eyes immediately grew double the actual size. I could see the lump in his throat when he swallowed his spit. My ego grew with each passing second as the fear radiated off Dino. In a swift motion Reggie whipped his burner out and put it to Dino's temple.

"Oh, you ain't talking now, huh?" I teased. "Bring yo' ass to the back." I motioned as I headed to the back of the club. It was so packed no one seemed to have noticed a whole kidnapping in the flesh.

"Where you going?" The stripper said, blocking my path. The 6'1" Amazon chick was built like a stallion, and her golden skin possessed this enchanting glow.

"Get out the way," I rudely demanded, effortlessly brushing past her. I hated when a bad bitch felt entitled because of her good looks. I respect women who respect themselves first and foremost. Like Gates say, *"She just high yella; she not that important."*

"Fuck you too!" She hollered out.

I didn't give a damn how she felt. I burst into the restroom instantly scoping for any witness, but to my surprise no one was pissy. "It's good, Reggie!" I called out holding the bathroom door open while Reggie and a staggering Dino followed suit.

Without warning I removed the .9 from my jeans and commenced to beating Dino's ass. *Whack!* The first hit to the back of his head dazed him. Whack! The second blow to the temple knocked Dino to his knees; zoned out but still on his knees. Dino's eye sockets must've been stretched to the capacity. They were unusually big. Drool fell from his slightly opened mouth. His unawareness forced him to look straight ahead while he remained erect on bended knees. *Whack!* Splattered blood landed on the door of the bathroom stalls. Once the third hit connected with Dino's mouth like a sack of potatoes he toppled face first, and like a hungry lion I leaped on top of him, hammering his head in repeatedly with the .9 millimeter. Pound for pound I kept going until I could see his skull peeking through the meat that covered his head. Dino was dead before I finished. I got a whiff of his piss and shit and struck him harder.

"Tim, that's enough, come on man!" Reggie yelled a bit hysterical.

Boom! The door to the restroom swung open, hitting the wall behind it. Chris rushed in. "What the fuck?" Chris looked mournful, but the thought quickly vanished once he whipped out his hammer with a silencer attached, then let off two shots in the side of Dino's head. "Gone, move 'round, Lil' Tim. I'll get this shit cleaned up." He assured standing over Dino's dead body.

I left the restroom without a single word spoken. Reggie stepped over Dino's body and I followed suit locking the B with Chris before exiting. Locking the B was a small handshake between Bloods as a form of greeting and a farewell.

"That bitch ass nigga act like he done did some," Reggie stated as we made our way back to VIP.

I smiled and shook my head at Reggie's remark. It was crazy how much he hated Chris. Bando was still in VIP doing him when me and Reggie walked up. "Where was yo antennas, nigga?" I inquired calmly flopping down next to Bando.

"I knew y'all niggas was over good. I had the bitch hemmed up. She say dude was invited." He informed, puffing on the Swisher.

"What chick?"

"The one he was talking to before you walked up. I walked up on the bitch. She claimed his fam invited him. She didn't know dude name, but she said she could point him out if she saw him," Bando continued, passing the blunt to Reggie.

"Fuck it. It don't matter. That nigga dead now. It's probably some broke ass nigga I don't even know. Come on. We 'bout to go fuck with Donk!" I stated, turning on my heels.

"Whaatt? We ain't been here that long," Bando whined throwing his arms up.

"Come yo' ass on. You done had your fun for the night," Reggie said, as he bypassed Bando.

***

The Buffalo Wild Wings was packed like the club. I spotted Donk and a corny, but paid looking, white dude at the bar. I led the way as Reggie, Bando and I headed to the bar. The pale faced waitress looked nothing like the bunnies at Hooters. A baseball game was on the plasma on the left side and the fight was on the right side with smaller screens around the center.

"What's up, baby?" I said sliding in between Donk and the white boy.

"Damn, 'bout time, nigga," he responded calmly. "What's up, Bando and Reggie? Y'all niggas have fun at the club?" He asked playfully. You could tell he had a little liquor in his system.

"Hell yeah," Bando answered first.

"It was alright," me and Reggie agreed in unison.

"Ooohhh." The white boy vocalized catching my attention. I watched the replay, instantly grimacing at the ruthless combination. "Pay up!" he shouted, slapping his hand against the wood on the bar.

"Alright, it ain't shit," Donk declared, pulling the bank roll from his pocket.

"Double or nothing?" Kyle questioned.

"Yeah, I got Ortiz."

"Oh you're crazy. That's a bet. I know for a fact Midlow will whoop his ass." He proclaimed confidently.

Damn, 30K on a fight? That's a lot of fucking money. I was sitting on a hundred grand but 30K would surely put a dent in that, I thought. "Donk, come here, man," I stated, walking off to the side.

Donk slowly stood to his feet but quickly made his way where I stood. "What's up, youngin?" He questioned, removing the expensive Cartier glasses.

"You good, nigga? That's 30K!" I was trying to see if Donk was too wasted for his own good.

"Fam...trust. I wouldn't have doubled the pot if I didn't know shit. Fuck a lot of money. Hell, it's too much money, but I've become addicted to this shit since them kids been gone. This like the sixth bet." He vented.

I could see the anguish in his eyes and couldn't do nothing but look away. "Alright, fam, I'm going to sit back and let you do your thing," I surrendered. Donk was more aware than ever.

Minutes passed and the fight began. The two men went at it like pit bulls. I hated those fights where they run around the ring for the first two rounds. They sprung into action round one. Me and Bando had our own bet going. Hundred dollars, whoever could down their shots of Henny the quickest. Reggie stayed on alert. I didn't expect anything other than that.

"Nigga, you cheated!" He shouted, nearly choking on his drink

"Nigga, the bet was drink three, not how to drink them," I protested. Bando was upset because I used one hand to drink two shots at once. "Run it!"

"Run me my cash, boy!" Donk continued with a huge grin on his face, standing to his feet.

"Dammit!" Kyle expressed, angrily banging his closed fist against the counter. Retrieving the $15,000 from each pocket he slowly handed it over to Donk. "I'll keep in touch" Kyle promised, walking off.

"Shots on me!" Donk bragged.

CHAPTER 14
PJ

The metallic blue door shut and my shoulders sank in defeat. I knew the murder would come back to haunt me. I just didn't think it would come so soon. Arianna had been on my mind heavy since my arrest. I felt like I was leaving her to fend for herself. Since witnessing her in the despicable act, I felt like it was my job to protect her. I felt more at ease after the visit with Donk after he assured me she'll be okay.

"If you want to participate in M.I. time, come out and take a seat in the dayroom!" The CO yelled. Not having a clue what M.I. was, I slid my feet in the brown crocs and slid out my cell. I could have easily asked my cellmate what was this "M.I" thing but Donk told me not to do much talking. Whenever you are talking, you can't hear. When you can't hear, a lot of times you can't see and to be aware is to be alive. You have to be observant. So , I didn't want to open the door for conversing at all. With my case, I had to steer clear of trouble and choose my associates wisely. One at a time, the boys filed out and the doors slammed. We were led to a smaller but spacious room with long wooden tables and metal chairs. A boat shaped clear cube was placed on one of the tables filled with the paper, pens and art supplies. I looked around confused but I assumed we were about to color or something, but what does M.I. stand for? "Gather whatever supplies you're using and have a seat" The CO instructed. When I turned around and got a good look at dude, I wanted to burst out laughing. He looked just like the comedian Dave Chapelle. I sat alone at a desk while the other boys mingled at the tables.

"Aye, y'all remember the girl we saw on the news for cutting that dude in Pleasant Grove?" One of the boys voiced out loud. I hadn't saw it on the news personally, but I had a strong feeling he was talking about Kadejah. He now had my undivided attention.

"Hell yeah, I remember, nigga." His friend responded taking his eyes off the paper in front of him.

"Well, I was at visitation the other day and me and her happen to have our visit the same day. Man, that bitch look better in person." He praised licking his lips. I slid out of the desk and mobbed over to the table where the boy sat. He was crispy black with a nappy afro.

"Say, bitch ass nigga. Watch how you speak on my sister!" I scolded through clenched teeth. The veins protruded from my arms as I hovered over him with closed fist.

"Nigga, fuck you. You bet—"

Before he could finish his shit talking, I took off. I threw left and right jabs, hitting him in his nose and chin until he hit the floor. To my surprise, the CO didn't intervene. I lifted my leg to stomp him but suddenly, I was picked up off of my feet. Without a fight, I calmly allowed the CO to restrain me. I knew I had messed up snapping on ol' boy, but I couldn't control it.

"Y'all done?" The CO asked, standing in the center of the room. The boy I had fought was struggling to stand to his feet. A few of his friends helped him to his chair.

"Yeah." I assured, smoothing the wrinkles from my shirt. A soft chuckle escaped his mouth as he turned on his heels to go back to his desk.

"Okay, y'all good. Go ahead and resume," he instructed.

Damn, that's it? I'm not going to get a case or no sort of trouble? I thought.

"Damn, bro. You connected the dots on his ass." The dark colored Hispanic boy praised sitting in the desk next to mine. "I would've done the same shit behind my little sister. You lucky to be in her life Me and my little sister were split up at birth. CPS took us from our mother because she was on dope real bad. My dad took me, but my sister wasn't his. He wasn't able to take her." He explained while fidgeting with his fingers.

"So, then what happened?" I inquired.

"She became a victim of the system, bouncing from one foster home to the next." He revealed.

"Damn, I couldn't imagine being split from Kadejah for so long. This shit right here killing me now." I confessed. "What's M.I.?" I continued.

"Miscellaneous time. You can write draw, color, do puzzles. Use whatever supplies and activities that in the bucket," he said. "I'm Fernando by the way."

"I'm PJ. How long have you been in here? I inquired, scribbling nothing in particular on the blank copy paper.

"Almost two months. I should be leaving in a week or two," He responded.

"Oh okay. That's what's up. What you in here for?" I asked suddenly anticipating his answer.

Me and this lil' freak at my school was having sex behind the building. She had this weird conclusion that if I stuck the X pill in her booty hole, she would feel it fast. So, I did just that. Minutes later after we finish, she start tripping. I ditched her ass and went to lunch with my boys. The next thing I know, the security guard and a policeman walk up to me and escort me out of the cafeteria. They searched my backpack and found the 30 X pills. Come to find out, she spilled the beans:" He explained, shaking his head.

Man, and I thought I was wild. This guy had me beat.

"Damn nigga, so you had 30 X pills? I asked, looking up at him. I followed his eyes and the boy I had just demolished was smirking at me, along with three of his friends. I knew that look all too well. These niggas was going to try to get at me. I never had to look over my shoulders in a situation that could result in me being harmed. Usually, it would be situations like staying up past curfew playing video games while turning the volume all the way down to zero and pressing the buttons on the controller softly so I wouldn't get caught, but this was one of those keep one eye open type of things. I didn't want Fernando to pick up on my uneasiness and mistake it for fear. I continued to ask questions. He did all the talking while I just listened. Donk also told me if talking was so imperative, we would've been blessed with two mouths instead of two ears.

An hour later, we were back in our dorm. Fernando stayed three cells down from me. I eyed homie closely until the CO slammed the door shut. I had been watching the op so intensely. It didn't dawn on to check out my roommate. The cushioned object covered my small head as I found it extremely difficult to breathe I grabbed what perceived to be a pillow, in attempt to remove the object from my face but his grip was bootyhole tight. Panic would only suffocate me quicker. I had to think fast. I was scared as hell. Tears of struggle, pain and fear damped the cotton. In one shift motion, I threw my legs over the side of the top bunk and without properly gripping the railing, I hit the concrete hard and fast. My kneecaps ached and had turned white from the impact of the harsh landing. Despite being in pain, I quickly rolled underneath the table right before the boy's foot connected with the side of my head. Surely enough, he was one of the boys who helped the op up.

"Get out from underneath the table, punk ass nigga!" he barked, bouncing on the top of his toes like he was Ali.

"You the punk. You got at me in my sleep, pussy!" I teased looking for a way out without getting hammered.

"Oh yeah, I'm a pussy?" He grinned, inching closer to the table. Like a thief in the night, I reached out and grabbed him by his ankle, yanking him towards me with all my might. Unable to balance himself on the opposite foot, he came crashing down like the Twin Towers. Landing flat on his back, his head hit the concrete and bounced off of it like a ping pong ball.

"Damn I hope this nigga ain't dead." I mumbled, lifting up off the floor. I hovered over his motionless body looking for movement when I noticed his chest rise and fall. Seeing that he was just unconscious, I kicked him in his jaw and twice in the ribs. I spit a lougy in his face before climbing onto my bunk. Minutes later, the CO came to my door and noticed the motionless boy sprawled out.

"What the fuck?" He asked opening the door. He quickly rushed inside and squatted beside him to check his pulse.

"He attacked me and I just defended myself, sir." I plead sitting up straight on my bunk.

"You lucky, I thought this boy was dead. I let you make it with one fight but your ass about to go to SEG." He rambled using the sink water to splash on the boy's face.

"Patterson, wake up!" He yelled, lightly slapping his face. Shortly after, Patterson came to.

"Step outside!" the CO ordered, meeting my gaze with fuming eyes. I backpedaled out of the cell looking around nervously for a way out but there was no use. Minutes later, the CO closed the door behind him and escorted me down the hallway to SEG. SEG held only six rooms.

"This you right here." He pointed to cell 4. He slammed the door shut and I was immediately brought to the realization I was in lock up, locked up. SEG was exceptionally quiet. Feeling sense-less, I scooted to the corner of the room and sat still. There were no mat, hygiene, not anything but a toilet and a sink and a mirror that resembled a cookie tray.

"Who that?" A voice called out. I stood to my feet to look out through the square shaped feeding slot that was on the metal door.

"What the hell?" Why you down here?" I asked Fernando, who was now looking through his hole as well.

"Baby T tried to come at me on some trip shit 'cause he felt like I took your side when you fought Busta." He stated unboth-ered.

"Y'all fought?" I asked.

"Yeah, I dropped that fool. I got down here like ten minutes before you showed up." He retorted. "Why you in here?" Fernan-do continued.

"I banged my roommate up. I guess he was one of Busta's friends, last name Patterson?" I pressed.

"Pee Wee, that's Pee Wee. You banged him up? That lil' nig-ga got something." He bragged.

"Well, like Rocco say, Good just ain't good enough." I quot-ed. Me and Fernando talked about all kinds of shit and rapped songs until we fell asleep.

Ah'Million

CHAPTER 15
PERSUASIA

I had been working nonstop at the hospital since everything with the kids went down. More and more people were being chopped down like trees. I was losing my cool. Witnessing the deaths, work was hectic and home was miserable. PJ and Kadejah were my pride and joy. They're absence was driving me insane. Arianna hadn't progressed, so l and Doctor Haynes to come check her out. She revealed that Arianna was still in a state of shock. Time should help, but it may be best if we admit her into a psychiatric hospital to make sure there's no further mental issues. If so, she can receive proper medication. The other day I took her to Timberland so they can monitor her daily activity. She would have to stay two to four weeks.

Donk is never home. When he's here, he's sleep. Lately, he been on the go and I'm too tired to keep up. He answer my calls, but damn where the love at? Tonight, I was going to the club to show Esha some love. I would throw a thousand ones on her to make the stunting ass niggas come out of they pockets. Niggas don't like to feel outdone, especially by a chick. Before you know it, it turns into a money throwing contest. Ella Mae's Shot Clock blasted through the TV speakers. The Ciroc had me feeling loose and sexy as I sang along to the words, snapping my fingers in the air to the beat; I took my time getting dressed. My Chanel bodysuit lay neatly across the bed with a new pair of Christian Loubitons. I sat on the edge of my bed, applying Jergens lotion to my skin when my phone vibrated on the dresser. Hoping it was Donk, my shoulders sagged in disappointment when I saw Esha's name flash across the screen.

"Hello?"

"Bitch, it don't even sound like you dressed!" Esha assumed.

"I'm getting dressed now, whore! What's up."

"Man, head out ASAP. I just pulled up 10 minutes ago and it's lit!"

"Okay, I'm leaving now. Give me twenty minutes." I replied, hanging up the phone, I threw the phone on top of the covers and snatched the bonnet off my head, using my long French manicured nails to comb through the loose waves. I lightly sprayed the tea tree oil sheen while softly shaking my head. My makeup was perfection. Instead of the natural colors, I went exotic with a silver cat eye, a little highlight on my cheeks and three coats of crimson red lipstick. I hummed and slid in my bodysuit. The expensive fabric clung to my body and hugged my curves. Sliding into the Christian Loutibitons, I grabbed my tennis bracelet and my platinum necklace with the five carat tear drop pendant before making my exit.

I pulled up to the King of Diamonds and it looked like a crime scene investigation going on.

"What the fuck?" I mumbled, pulling my phone out of the Balenciaga clutch.

"Esha?"

"Persuasia!" She yelled into the phone. "The laws everywhere. Someone was killed. Meet me at the Shell's right off the freeway."

"Okay."

I slowly looked around the lot before peeling out. The laws were so deep that I couldn't catch a glimpse of nothing. I was able to see a shoe. It was a heel that lay abandoned on top of the gravel. The red and blue lights illuminated the dark street and I decided I had seen enough. The Shell gas station was a whole different kind of scenery. You would've thought everyone from the club was posted up here. The lights were bright, lot was full, music loud. The sight of it all made me anxious and I couldn't wait to hop out and feel all eyes on me. I parked beside the air pump since all the parking spaces were occupied. Esha appeared out of nowhere, waving her hand and approaching the passenger side of my black Range Rover. I killed the engine and climbed out slowly and seductively, just in case eyes were on me. Sure enough, they were. The niggas had the females beat tonight and at the moment, all eyes were on me and Esha.

"Bitch, you look good!" Esha yelled, enthused to see me.

"Preciate ya, you do too, girl." I complimented. Esha wore a long sleeve, black Versace dress that barely covered her phat ass. "Uh uh, bitch. It's way too many niggas out there." I continued while me and Esha headed inside of the gas station.

"It's cool, we about to head out." She stated before walking inside of the store.

"Hi ladies," The clerk called out from behind the counter.

"Heeyy." Esha spoke dragging out the three-letter word. I just flashed a smile and kept it moving. We were in and out in no time, only to be met by a red Maserati parked out front. The dark tint was hiding the face of the person behind the wheel.

"Who is that?" Esha asked, squinting her eyes trying to peer inside. Before I could utter a word, the Lamborghini doors flew upwards on both sides. Both dudes smoothly climbed out of the vehicle. The driver caught my attention by surprise. His swag was official. No bullshit, no mediocre shit. He was saying something and his friend looked good too. Dressed in Gucci from head to toe, I knew right then it wasn't anything average about them. My mind was screaming run, but my legs wouldn't move. I shifted my weight to one side and placed my hand on my hip while clutching the Shell bag and my clutch in the opposite hand.

"Damn! Where y'all headed?" Esha questioned once the dudes were in ear shot.

"Trying to see if we could spend some time with y'all' beautiful ladies." The driver said, exposing his pearly whites. He licked his succulent lips after he stated his motive and it made my pussy throb. I couldn't believe I was actually standing here feeling like this behind another dude. No guy since meeting Donk has caught my eye. No one tempted me in more ways than one like this.

"Oh nah, we good." I replied walking in between the dudes heading in the direction of my truck. I bit down on my lip to help refrain from doing something I'll regret. I looked over my shoulder and spotted Esha in the same spot. I just rolled my eyes and shook my head, but hey I couldn't be upset with Esha. She was single.

"Wait, Persuasia. Hold on!" Esha yelled while coming after me. I stopped Esha dead in her tracks before she could even finish.

"Hell nah, bitch! You already know I'm not with that shit. You disrespecting not only me but my relationship and my nigga."

"But P." She begged, grabbing my arm.

"Nah, P shit. You out of line." I fumed while snatching away.

"P, I explained your situation and told them I'll do it alone, but they don't want one without the other. P, I need the money. You got a nigga who tends to your every need. I'm still that same bitch living a day to day trying to make it." She whined trying to look all distressed and shit.

"Where the fuck is Hennessey at? That's yo' bitch, ain't it?" I mocked.

"She left the club with this nigga from Detroit. He paying her to accompany him for the night."

"Please P, I promise I won't ask you again. Matter of fact, I won't even tell you to swing by the club again. Period."

I rolled my eyes, not wanting to tell my friend no but not wanting to give in either.

"They already have everything set up. They just need two private dancers." Esha stated.

"Look ladies, we from Atlanta. This my brother and we're on a business trip. We want to enjoy ourselves on our last night in your city." He confessed.

"P. He doesn't have to know. Come on, just two hours. I'm Kareem and this is Markeif." Kareem chimed in.

"They outsiders! Persuasia, what's the big deal?" She asked a bit frustrated.

"I don't know about his one, Esha" I stated with my arms crossed.

"Man, it's been years since we hit that stage together. Can we just do it this one time for the last time?" She begged. My shoulders dropped and I smacked my lips before agreeing.

"Alright, this one time and one time only."

I imagined everything would

be set up in a small cramped up room since we were dealing with out of town cats, but I was wrong. I entered the spacious two-bedroom condo. The lack of furniture made the condo look twice its actual size. A black leather sectional was placed at the head of the living room, an oval shaped table was directly in the middle and a sixty-inch plasma decked the wall. A few African culture paintings hung on the opposite side. On the other end of the living room were two shiny stripper poles. The condo smelled liked Febreeze and Downy detergent. The sight of the place alone stunned me. I just couldn't see men of their caliber to live like this. Nothing seemed to have been out of place. Esha wasted no time getting comfortable, sitting her oversized MK bag on the couch, and walking up to the pole.

"We got all kinds of alcoholic and non-alcoholic beverages. Make yourself at home." Kareem stated heading down the hallway. Markeif plopped down on the sofa retrieving a shoebox lid from underneath. He was definitely the quiet one.

"Oh, okay, they set it up right." Esha admitted yanking on the pole to ensure it was secure.

"Y'all must do this often because it took me forever to figure out the correct way of getting the pole to hook up." She teased.

"That doesn't matter. Y'all are here right now." He responded, stunning the hell out of me. *Ol' cocky ass.* I dropped my Hermes bag onto the coffee table and preceded in the direction of the kitchen. Guilt was kicking in and I was bout ready to go. I opened the fridge and spotted a few beers, vitamin waters, couple bottles of Dasani, six pack of Gatorades, a 2 liter of big Peach, and sat it on the countertop. I checked all the other cabinets until discovered the right one. It was every bottle you could think of. It took me sometime but I discovered the Peach Ciroc behind the Crown Royal Black. I immediately grabbed the Styrofoam cups from the pantry and made me and Esha a drink. Kareem had made his way from the back. A bottle of Henny in one hand and a box of swishers in the other.

"Oh, you holding out on the Hen?" I playfully asked Kareem as he bypassed me. He paused before backing up to where I stood.

"Nah, never that. It's a bottle under there too. I'm just trying to keep a few extra bottles of my favorite tucked away." He admitted before dropping his head and proceeding to the living room.

"These motherfuckas." I mumbled carrying me and Esha's drink in each hand.

"Esha!" I called out standing in the middle of the living room. Kareem was scanning through the YouTube videos on the smart TV, while Markeif rolled blunts, chuckling at something on his phone. They engaged in frivolous conversation for what felt like minutes before they noticed me watching them.

"Where's Esha?" I asked. On the cool, he really caught me staring. I'm sure locating Esha wasn't a problem. It's not like we were in a mansion.

"Oh, she in the restroom. Y'all almost ready? I overheard y'all talking and since all we have is two hours, I really want to get to the entertainment." He expressed, slowly eyeing me from top to bottom.

I smirked because I could only imagine how he'll react once I peel these clothes off.

The restroom was connected to the bedroom. The bedroom was simple but neatly organized.

"Esha, here girl." I called out as I waited for her to open the door. Esha snatched the door open. Powder residue was still on the tip of her nose.

"Thanks, bitch. What's this?" She inquired taking the drink from my hand. She threw it back and in two gulps it was gone.

"You still fucking with that shit I see." I said, sipping on my drink watching her intensely.

"Come on, Persuasia. Don't start that bullshit. I don't have time for a speech. Hey! I got an extra fit for you to dance in and if you like, you can wear these Balenciaga thigh highs. That's if you don't want to wear your red bottoms." She offered, fixing the strands on her head that hung loosely.

"Okay, this fit goes better with my red bottoms, but those thigh highs are sexier. I'm trying to put these niggas in a trance." I responded, finishing my drink. I removed my clothes and put on the extensively revealing, but erotic, baby doll pink, two-piece with the smoke gray and black boots. Esha wore a lime green and lavender fit with the clear six-inch pumps.

"Let's go make this money, bitch."

I slightly twisted the knob on the wall to dim the lights, startling both men. Their head quickly snapped in our direction. I threw my long hair over my shoulders, placing my other clothes in my Hermes bag. The honey godly body butter had my skin glistening like a full moon and my eyes never left Kareem.

"I see y'all ready." Kareem stated as he passed me and Esha, only to return carrying eccentric shaped, yet expensive looking chairs. The chairs were black and looked to be made out of metal, but the seat of it sunk low. A feather like cushion decorated the back. Markeif grabbed the two Fila shoe boxes that were positioned on the table and quickly took his seat a few feet away in front of the pole that Esha was stationed at. Kareem followed suit, scooting one of the shoe boxes closer to him.

"Oh shit, I forgot about the music. Look, this is our preferred play list. Just tell me fast or slow." He spoke as the blunt dangled from his lip. I could tell by the aroma that it was Kush. OG to be exact.

"Tonight is about y'all, so it's all on you. Play whatever you want to see us shake this ass too." Esha stated, winking at me. My nerves got so bad once he pulled the playlist up. I ran to the table and took a swig of the Henny from the bottle.

Please Me by Cardi B and Bruno Mars blasted through the speakers. I looked at Esha and smiled. *How did I know this nigga was going to play this song?* I thought. Like pros, me and Esha got to it like it was nothing to it. She did her thing and I did mine. Detaching myself from the pole, I slowly and seductively walked up to Kareem while removing my top. The cold temperature had my nipples on hard. In one swift motion, I threw my top at him and it landed perfectly on his bald fade. Once I got close enough, I turned and grabbed my ankles while making my ass clap. I could feel him stuffing bills into my thong, which only made me go harder. Turning back around to face him, I positioned his legs closer together, put my head in between his legs. I was using his legs and using my upper strength to secure myself. He was now face to face with my round ass. I pointed my toes in and out which enabled my thighs to move in a slow steady but entrancing motion. I felt Kareem place a soft pecks on my booty cheeks and it sent chills down my spine.

Using my ass to give him a round of applause, I moved to the beat. He caressed the back of my calves, down to my ass cheeks while stuffing bills in the band around my thigh, upper arm and thong. Safely landing on my feet, I straddled Kareem. The song Work Out by Wale and Megan thee Stallion kicked in and each cheek jumped with the beat. Right, left, left, right, right. I did this a couple more times as if I was throwing a combination. I looked to my right over at Esha and Markeif practically had his whole finger in her pussy while she was bent over in front of him twerking. I made my way back to the pole and did a few of my famous tricks. We continued to entertain the best way we knew how, which wasn't complicated by far. We took quick breaks in between to take a few tokes on the blunt and drink a shot of whatever, but the night had to come to an end. It just ended in a way I hadn't planned.

CHAPTER 16
KADEJAH

The same routine every day. It had been a little over two weeks since my arrest and I was beginning to feel content. I honestly didn't have a clue why I was feeling this way but I am. I'd written PJ three times, yet still no response. I called Uncle Donk a few days ago and he informed me on Arianna's whereabouts. I really hoped she would pull through so we can be one big happy family.

"It's chow time, line up!" Ms. Smith yelled standing by the door. Chow was practically the same thing every day. I was beginning to enjoy the mystery meat. In orderly fashion, we lined up. Me, Tru, Shun, and Kedra. Over the past few days, me and Tru had gotten exceptionally close. I shared past memoires, few deep secrets, my dreams and aspirations and she did the same. She was like a friend, sister and diary all in one. The smell of the food made my mouth water as we stood in a single file line against the wall. From where I stood, I could see the other dorm lining up for chow as well. We ate our meal in the same setting where we had M.I. time.

"You going to give me your mystery meat? I asked Tru, looking straight ahead. "Huh?" I continued once I didn't hear a response. I finally turned around to see Tru tucking her pants into her sock. "Tru?" I called out hovering over her.

"What? I got to fix my swag." She declared with a boyish grin revealing that gap in between her two front teeth. I turned back around, shaking my head playfully.

G wing was now lined up directly across from us. G Wing held females our age and two to three years older. A lot of them had mean scowls on their face, but none of them intimidated me. One of the chicks was fully developed. Breast and ass. Her body almost resembled Persuasia's. She had a caramel complexion and a nose that looked odd. Her lips looked like two number two pencils stacked on top of one another and her hair was shoulder length but in need of a relaxer. She looked at me with attitude and rolled her eyes, but her eyes also remained glued on Tru.

"Come on, Richards and get his tray!" Ms. Smith yelled. I hadn't even realized the line had moved so quickly. I walked up to the trustee, a trusted inmate, grabbed my tray and walked inside the M.I. room before giving the chick one last glance before finding a seat. Me, Kedra, Shun and Tru had our own table. Tru walked in shortly after me. Before I could utter a word to Tru, the girl from G Wing walked in with her tray and sits at the table directly across from us.

"So, this you, Tru?" She asked in a low tone looking in my direction.

"Bruh, I don't fuck with you!" Tru shot back focusing her attention back on her food.

I looked from the girl and then back to Tru while I tore into my mystery meat.

"Y'all roommates? Y'all fucking?" She asked with a venomous stare.

"Bitch why? Keep my name out your mouth foreal, foreal." I stated rolling my eyes.

"Who you talking to? I'll whoop your ass. You don't know me." She stated getting up out of her seat.

With a quickness, I hopped to my feet as well.

"Bitch, what you doing?" Tru asked with wide eyes, pulling up her pants to the middle of her mid-section.

"Chill, y'all." Kedra and Shun reasoned pulling on me and Tru.

"Whatever you want to do, bitch, I'm ready." I voiced, looking into her eyes. The girl turned on her heels, and I turned as well to take a seat.

"Kadejah!" Shun yelled but it was too late. Tru's old chick had tried to sneak me from behind, but Tru caught her with a left hook to the jaw causing her to stumble back. I walked up on the action as the two went at it. Shun stayed by my side with her hand in front of my stomach so I wouldn't jump in. It was useless cause if I decided to jump in, she or anyone else wouldn't be able to stop me. The chick was no match for Tru. Tired of fading the haymakers that Tru was throwing her way, she reached out and latched on to Tru's hair with both hands in attempt to pull her down. Two swift uppercuts snapped her neck backwards, forcing her to crash into the table a few feet away.

"Everybody move!" The CO yelled as he barged in. The small crowd that had formed parted like the Red Sea as the extremely tall bald guy led the way of his comrades with cuffs in his hand. Tru had caught her breath and was ready for round two. When she heard the dude's voice, she slowly raised her hands in mock surrender.

"Where you going, Tru?" I asked while the CO placed the cuffs around her wrist.

"I'm going to SEG. And from there, I'll get moved to a different dorm." She responded. Her hair was a bit disheveled and before I was able to utter another word, she dropped her head in dismay while being led out of the room.

Once we were escorted back to the dorm, everyone was lit and discussing the fight. A few girls were even demonstrating a few moves Tru used on the girl.

"Man, Tru gave Brooke's ass the business." Shun commented, leaning against the cubby holders.

"Oh, that's her name?" I rhetorically asked keeping my eyes on the door, hoping Tru would walk through it.

"Yeah, they used to mess around when she used to stay in this dorm before she was moved to G Wing." Shun informed.

"Her and Tru snuck and had sex once or twice when Ms. Smith was on the phone." She continued.

"What do you mean snuck?" I repeated with one of my brows raised.

"Well, they weren't technically roommates. Tru was allowed permission to go inside to get her mail, because we were scheduled for M.I. in an hour. Well, Brooke snuck in while Ms. Smith was on the phone. It was an outside call. Something was going on at home."

"Um." I groaned folding my arms feeling a bit jealous, which I'll never admit to Shun.

"Girl, quit worrying about Tru and let me do something to that pretty hair of yours." She insisted, grabbing her comb out the cubby holder. Without a verbal fight, I willingly sat down in the empty seat. I truly missed Tru more and more with each passing second. I looked left across the room at Kedra and a few other girls who were still discussing the fight. All I could do was laugh. Kedra was truly a character. Shun parted my hair into tiny pieces and scratched my cap. By the time she was done, I was damn near asleep. She took her small hands and massaged it thoroughly, carefully caressing my temples. It was as if I was in a life of bliss. My eyes shut and all my body parts became numb.

"That feel good, huh?" Shun asked. I could feel her breath on my ear.

"Mmmm hmmm," I groaned, afraid drool would escape my lips if I allowed them to part.

"Okay, it's time for me to braid it now." She announced combing through it.

"I'm tender headed." I informed sitting up straight. Bracing myself for the braids, I allowed my mind to drift off. Somehow, I was going to find my way to Tru once she gets out of Seg. That's if she wants me to. Yeah, it was her fault the girl came at me the way she did, but she had my back and front 100%.

"Oww! That hurt, Shun." I whined jerking my head forward.

"Okay, cry baby. I'll be light." Shun quipped

Several minutes had passed and there was still no sign of Tru. Although the windows were exceedingly small, I could see the sun starting to set.

"So, Kadejah, I just want to know. Why did you do it?" Shun asked.

"Do what?" I asked dumbfounded.

"Why you cut the dude?" She snooped.

"I only did it because he hit my brother and hurt my sister. She's having issues right now because of that shit!" I ranted.

"There's loopholes. Just explain it all from the beginning." She insisted and that I did.

Two days had passed since I saw Tru and I was missing her like crazy. I was hoping to receive good news from Steve that will relieve this feeling of depression. I followed the male CO through the vestibule area and down the steps.

"I got one on her way to the 7th floor. She's going to G Wing." The female officer announced. I couldn't see her face because she remained around the corner. My heartbeat sped up and I instantly became anxious to see who awaited on the other side.

"Okay, I just have one headed to visitation. You can bring her around." He stated, shifting me to the left so whoever it was could easily bypass. My assumption was correct. Tru hit the corner with her bag in hand. I knew that walk from anywhere.

"Tru." I called out. Her head shot up. The wrinkles vanished and her scowl was replaced with a huge smile.

"I love you, Kadejah." She expressed with her face now serious. The sentimental words caught me off guard.

"Quit talking and come on!" The CO yelled, yanking my arm. My body jerked but I didn't feel a thing. I was deep in reverie once Tru spoke those words. Further apart and right before she was completely out of sight, I mouthed the words. I love you too. I was intending to say them aloud, but I guess my speakers busted. Either way, Tru got the message, seeing that she flashed me that boyish grin right before I turned the corner. I stumbled over my own feet as the CO continued to yank on my arm. I was hoping this was Uncle Donk or Lil Tim coming with Steve to visit me. So I can snitch on his lame ass.

"Y'all know the procedure. Find a room and stand next to it." He demanded, releasing his grip as he removed the cuffs.

"Bitch ass nigga." I mumbled while walking off.

"What you say?" The CO asked through squinted eyes.

"If you heard me, why you asking?" I challenged without slowing my stride.

"Oh you a tough one, huh?" He chuckled rubbing his goatee. The visitors came pouring in and my eyes remained locked on the CO. This dude really thought he was tough. We locked eyes and he flashed me a shady grin. Steve came through the door and I tried my best to disguise how I felt but Steve read me like a book.

"You okay, Kadejah?" He asked looking around.

"Yeah, I'm okay, Steve. Did Uncle Donk or Lil Tim come with you?" I asked looking past him.

"No not today, Kadejah. This may be my last time." He smiled motioning me inside the room.

"Are you serious?" I asked, taking a seat.

"Yes, we reviewed the evidence at a hearing I scheduled with the judge and it was clearly self-defense. Arianna is in a psychiatric hospital due to the incident. My fight is the state or condition you would've been in if you hadn't done what you did," he explained. "There's only one problem..."

"What's that, Steve?" I inquired.

"Stop discussing your case with those females. The only thing that saved you from this informant turning state evidence is the fact that your entire case was recorded.

"Informant?" I thought aloud.

"Yes, someone who's working with the courts. They're either hired or they volunteer information to get a better deal on their own case." He informed. The first person that came to mind was Tru. I had told her everything without leaving out a single detail.

"Do you know a La'Shuna Wooten?" He asked resting his hands on the table.

"La'Shuna?" I repeated clearly.

"Yes."

"Shun, that bitch, Shun!" I yelled infuriated slamming my fist down on the table. I can't believe that bitch would try and play with my life like that.

"Oh, I guess. She goes by Shun in there?" Steve asked curiously.

"Yeah, she's a girl in my dorm. I thought we were cool. I honestly thought she could be trusted." I responded. I should've listened to Tru. She told me that bitch was a grimy liar. I was wrong to ever believe Tru would do something so foul. I sat there enraged as my left leg wobbled.

"Oh yeah, in case we have to go to court, your victim won't be able to testify. He was found dead a few days ago." Steve informed. I placed my hand over my mouth in astonishment.

"Don't ask how. I do not know, but what I do know is you need to keep your nose clean. If everything go as planned, you'll be released in three days." Steve stated standing to his feet. Still in shock, I nodded in approval. I sat in my cell contemplating on how I would get Shun. I hadn't been to my dorm to see if I was coming to the dayroom, but I calmly declined. Steve's words replayed heavy in my mind over and over.

Keep your nose clean.

I wanted so badly to walk away from it all and let vengeance be the Lord's like my pastor would say, but I wasn't to that point yet. Since Tru was now in G Wing, no one had yet to move in my cell with me. The girl Brooke was so banged up they gave her a facility transfer. Me and Tru had been exchanging mail through the trustee at chow and clean up time. It was evident. We missed one another and detested the separation. I peered over at the toothbrush on the sink and thought about stabbing this bitch and going all the way, but it was going to be impossible to sharpen the dull object to my liking. I do know I can kill two birds with one stone if I beat this bitch up, because I'll go to G Wing with Tru and receive instant gratification.

"Kedra!" I yelled out of the mesh on my door. Her and Shun both came. I rolled my eyes when I saw Shun coming towards my door.

"What's up?" Kedra asked with Shun in tow.

"Tell Ms. Smith I'm ready to come out." I responded. Shun didn't try hiding her excitement. She even jumped up and down a few times.

"I'm so glad you coming out. We got a lot to catch up on." She voiced flashing a huge grin.

Yeah, I'm glad I'm coming out too. I thought. I can't believe she could snake me behind my back and still smile in my face like she has done me no wrong. This chick was sleazy. A few minutes passed and Ms. Smith came and unlocked my door. Like a caged animal, I yawned while stretching after exiting my cell. Shun and Kedra sat in their usual seats and I sat in mine. I could tell the other girls were staring at me to see if I was distraught after everything that had taken place with Tru. The rumor around the detention center was Tru and I had been having sex when we were roommates. Ms. Smith was occupied on the phone as usual.

"Damn, what's up stranger?" Kedra quipped combing the naps out of her hair. I wondered if she was a part of Shun's little scheme against me.

"Shit, chilling, I had to get my mind right." I commented slowly scanning they dayroom, monitoring everyone's movement.

"I saw Tru at medical this morning. She told me to tell you she loves you and to try and get moved to G Wing." Kedra relayed slyly grinning. Hearing Tru's name alone sent me into a frenzy. Shun smacked her lips and reclined into her seat.

"Problem?" I asked with attitude.

"Nah, Kadejah, I just feel like its selfish of her to ask you that when she knows the only way you can get over there is if you get in trouble." She responded trying to sound sincere.

Bitch, what you know about trouble? Fucking with you, I'll be under the prison. I thought.

"Alright, let's drop the topic." I stated turning back around in my seat.

"So, how did your attorney visit go yesterday?" Shun pried.

"My what!" I turned around peering at her through squinted eyes.

"Your attorney visit." She repeated.

"How do you know it was my attorney?" I asked slowly standing to my feet.

"I mean because—"

Tooh!

With all the mucus at the rear of my throat, I hocked a loogy into Shun's face. I watched it slowly descend down her eyelashes and onto her nose where it toppled down to her lips. Flashing on her foulness, I rained blow after blow on her face. She tried to get up but her effort was useless. I could hear screaming all around me. I even heard fainted chants, something like "Whoop that bitch!" and "You better not fall!"

I couldn't make out who's voice was who. I didn't care to know either. Shun tried using her arms to shield her face, but her fragile barrier was no match for my powerful combinations. Blood squirted from the mouth and coated her teeth as she groaned in pain.

A powerful force from behind shoved me off Shun sending me crashing onto the floor. I looked up to see the same guy that was talking shit at visitation. Using the palm of his hand, he shoved the side my head into the tile floor.

"Get off me!" I yelled, kicking my feet. Without responding, he locked the handcuffs around my wrist. They were so tight that I could feel the metal piercing my skin. I wanted to cry out, but it would be pointless no one could hear me. Not PJ, Lil Tim or Uncle Donk.

A few days had passed but the scenery hadn't changed. I sat in the empty tank they called Seg. Seg had seven cells and at the moment, I occupied one of the seven. I received mail from Steve last night informing me that I'll be released sometime tomorrow. I was excited, nonetheless. I was a bit upset because I wanted to see Tru before I put this place behind me. My once tight and neat braids were now loose and frizzy. I felt like shit. I hadn't brushed my teeth or washed my ass. I wasn't allowed neither necessity.

"Richards." A voice called out. I hopped off the metal bunk, nearly tripping over my feet trying to rush out the door. I got up only to see the same guy that threw me on the ground and handcuffed me. He stood in front of my cell with a half smirk. This time I noticed the name tag.

"Woods." I scanned.

"Why the fuck they always send you to escort me?" I yelled. With tight lips, he squeezed the bridge of his nose.

"Say, just shut the fuck up and come on." He stated unlocking the cell door. Mr. Woods tightly gripped my arm and led the way. Mr. Woods wasn't an old peon. He was young. A young punk. I couldn't stand his ways, but I couldn't deny the fact he was sexy.

A thought that would remain in my mental. He rocked a bald fade. It wasn't high, but It wasn't real low either. No facial hair just a little chin hair. His brows were thick, and his lashes were long. His mocha colored skin and kissable lips were hot. He had lips like the NBA star Anthony Davis. He stood about 6'2" between 150 and 160 pounds.

"Can you loosen your grip, please?" Without responding, he loosened his grip surprisingly. The walk down the off-white hallway was unusually quiet. I was a bit embarrassed thinking he could smell my body odor through my clothes. I had just remembered I hadn't brushed my teeth, so I made a mental note to stop talking shit. We reached the elevators when a lady inside of an office walked out with a file.

"File for Kadejah Richards?" Mr. Woods asked.

"Yes, they notified me and told me to be expecting you." She responded flirtatiously. Quickly dismissing the bad weave wearing officer, we stepped into the elevator. Mr. Woods intensely read my file and his facial expressions deeply frustrated me. I tried standing on the tips of my toes and stretching my neck, but it was no use. The curiosity was killing me, and he knew that.

Bing.

The elevator opened. Mr. Woods was motionless, only moving his eyes as he continued to read. I slightly jerked, diverting his attention.

"Be still. I know this is our stop." He spoke harshly. I smacked my lips and remained stagnant. "Come on." He demanded, stepping off the elevator where he completely released his grip.

"Gone over there to G Wing with ya' little girlfriend." He mumbled walking ahead of me. He handed my file to one of the female COs that stood in the hallway. Hygiene bag covered the table where the officers sat. I grabbed a bag and made my way to G Wing. I peeked over my shoulders one more time and just as I predicted, Mr. Woods was keenly watching me. He didn't even bother to look away once we locked eyes.

What's up with this dude? I thought pressing the button that opens G Wing's door. I spotted Tru immediately, who was seated by the cubby holders. She was in the back at a circle shaped wooden table with two more girls. Her eyes bucked with excitement when she saw me walk through the door. Ms. King looked up from the desk and announced my assigned cell.

"Go to eight."

"Lytrice Oshae, where are you?" Ms. King called out looking around the dark room.

"I'm right here, Ms. King." Tru answered.

"This is your new roommate. Show her the proper way to make her bed." Ms. King stated.

"Yes, ma'am." She quickly answered.

In complete bliss, I hurried and followed Tru to cell eight. Since our split up, all I wanted was for us to link up. For us to be roommates again, that shit was exclusive. Once we were inside, Tru quickly shut the door and tightly embraced me. I hugged her back as if she was a long lost relative that I hadn't saw in years.

"I missed you, Kadejah." She leaned back without releasing her grip.

"I missed y—"

Tru stuck her tongue down my throat, and without hesitation, I kissed her back and for a second our tongues intertwined. Soft moans escaped my mouth and I didn't want it to end. Her pink lips were smaller than mine. However, they were a nice size and soft like pillows. She began to suck on my bottom lip Secured in her embraced and loving the feel of her lips against mine, she took me to a place of complete tranquility. Finally letting go, I backed away.

"Tru, I haven't brushed my teeth." I confessed.

"Girl, I don't care. I missed you. I love you." She admitted gazing into my eyes.

"My breath don't stink?" I asked feeling insecure about my stink breath.

"I told you I don't care!" She yelled frustrated. Damn, she really do care about me. I perked up my lips to the tip of my nose. Without saying another word, I grabbed my toothbrush and toothpaste and brushed my teeth. Tru just watched me from the side and smile. She climbed on top of the bunk and made my bed

"Look, you take the bottom I'm going to get on the top. If Ms. King ask why we switched, just say you fell and I decided to switch with you." Tru suggested. "So I heard you whooped Shun." She quipped. I turned away from the sink to face her and she wore that boyish grin. I could feel the butterflies at the pit of my stomach. The facial expression at this very moment always made me feel some type of way and she knew that.

"Like she was the stepchild." I shot back and Tru erupted with laughter.

"Girl, you hell. Show me how you whooped her ass." She joked, throwing punches like she was Floyd Mayweather.

"No Tru, just know I whooped the bitch." I bragged.

"The what?" She asked as if she didn't her what I said.

"The bitch." I repeated. Laughter filled the cell again. I just smiled and continued taking my hair down over the sink.

"Come on, I'll do it." She insisted, climbing down off the top bunk. I sat backwards on the toilet while Tru took my hair down. We talked and laughed for what felt like minutes but the approaching dark skies told me it had been hours. I still hadn't told Tru about my visit with Steve. At one point I actually forgot, because we were having so much fun and I didn't want to perturb her mood. Tru sat crisscross on the floor in front of me, while I sat on the toilet facing her. I listened to her closely as she told another one of her stories. Ms. King walked by for count and proceeded on.

"So, we in this Honda and we all the way out in—"

"Tru." I chimed in a low tone, looking down at my lap.

"Yeah, what's up?"

I deeply exhaled before responded.

"What's wrong, Kadejah?" she asked.

"I had a visit with Steve the other day, Tru."

"That's good. What did he say?" She replied dearly enthused. I lifted my head and gazed into Tru's eyes for just a brief moment.

"What he say?" Tru begged.

"I'm going home tomorrow, Tru!" I yelled out in frustration. Knowing the effect of the bomb I just dropped upset me knowing it would bother her. Tears slowly fell from my eyes and crocodile tears formed in Tru's. It was the first time I had seen her cry, and the look on her face only made me feel pitiful. Two weeks ago, I'd be laughing and kicking it, counting down the hours, but my life had changed since then and so did my feelings.

"Damn, I would've thought we was going to have a little more time together, but you leaving is a good thing." She admitted wiping the tears before they fell.

"It's just unexpected, that's all. I'm right behind you, boo." She assured lightening my damp spirit.

"Okay." I chuckled in between tears.

"That's right, Stanka. Tears of joy come here." She stated, standing to her feet. I walked into her open arms and melted. Strange to say, I hadn't rather been anywhere else than where I was at this very moment.

"Kadejah." she called out.

"Huh?" I responded.

"You gone fuck with me when you get out?"

"Of course, Tru." I replied looking into her eyes.

"We'll see. I've heard it before. Just know, if you don't my first day home, I'm gunning for you. I promise you that." Tru guaranteed.

"You believe me, don't you?" She continued using her index finger to lift my chin. I met her gaze. Our bodies were so close to one another that I could feel her warm breath. The lack of space in between us made me tense up a bit, but I was anxious more than anything. I nodded my head in approval instead of just simply saying yes. At that moment, the simple had become difficult because my mental was so far gone.

She lifted my hands up above my head and pulled my shirt off, tossing it to the side. Things begin to speed up once I realized we were about to actually take it there. I grabbed her face and shoved my tongue in her mouth. She kissed me back passionately and it was as if we were attacking one another with our lips. The room was filled with moans and grunts while we quickly undressed. Before assuming the position, Tru stepped back and gaped at me from head to toe with lustful eyes.

"Lay down." She demanded and with the quickness, I lay on top of the cemented floor. Using her legs to spread mine apart, she slid comfortable on her stomach. Like a fresh breath of air, she inhaled the scent of my treasure box.

"You smell good." She whispered right before she dived in. She planted soft wet kisses on you outer lips and licked around and between my slit. The euphoric feeling forced me to spread my legs wider allowing Tru more access to do her thing. She swiftly and constantly flickered her tongue across my love button and the unfamiliar, yet pleasant feeling forced me to arch my back in response.

"Tru." I moaned as if I wanted her to stop and acknowledge me but the last thing I wanted was for her to stop. My moans grew louder. I thought I would scream. I used both hands to cover my face and muffle out the sounds. Everything ceased so I quickly removed my hands from my face and before I could protest, Tru rubbed her finger against my opening before sliding it in.

"Aaahhhh." I deeply inhaled as she made her way inside of me. I scowled at the temporary twinge, which was quickly replaced with gratification. She moved her fingers around inside of me, touching places I never knew existed. Pure ecstasy is what I felt and I didn't want it to end.

"You like that, Kadejah?" She asked gazing up at me with those beautiful eyes.

"Yes." I whispered. She slowly eased down and started attacking my button with her tongue while she plunged her finger in and out of me. I gripped her ponytail and clenched my teeth to control my outburst. I couldn't help but move my hands from her head and began to claw at the floor.

"Oooohh, Tru." I cried out breathing heavy. My body began to shiver and I couldn't fathom what was occurring. The shivering became uncontrollable. My thighs snapped shut limiting Tru's movement.

"Aaargghh." I roared no longer being able to control my excitement. Tru quickly jumped to her feet.

"Girl, you going to get us in trouble." Tru stated looking out of the mesh. I lay motionless on the floor giggling. It wasn't even anything funny but I felt exceptionally satisfied. All I could do was laugh.

"Come on, Kadejah. Get up so we can lay up." Tru whispered. I slowly stood to my feet and went to the sink to wash off. Tru sat on the bunk and watched me the whole time. I put on my underclothes and cuddled underneath the sheets with Tru.

"Next time, I'm going to put a sock in your mouth." Tru quipped. We laughed and talked until four AM. I couldn't believe someone of the same sex could make me feel the way I felt. To connect on a mental and emotional level, only to feel the same high sexually, had me in a place of complete elation. The next morning I awoke to Tru shaking my shoulder.

"Huh?" I asked rubbing my eyes.

"Wake up." Ms. King walking around opening doors for breakfast." I quickly hopped up and got dressed while Tru used the sink. I got myself together once she was done.

"Y'all eating?" Ms. King asked waiting by the door.

"Yes, ma'am." We answered in unison.

G Wing was different than F Wing. I just clinged to Tru the whole time. She was a bit despondent and I knew I was the cause.

"Tru, what's wrong?" I asked as we made our way from breakfast.

"Nothing." She shot back, concentrating on the cemented floor.

"Tru." I called out grabbing her arm to slow her pace.

"What, Kadejah? I'm okay. I'm just going to miss you and it's not like I'm going to be able to call you or." She expressed shifting her hand up and down her braids.

"Tru, I know, and it's going to be okay because when they let you out, I'm going to be right there at the gate." I promised.

"Kadejah, go ahead and get your things together so you can get processed out." Ms. King announced.

"Already?" I asked in disbelief.

"Yes, what's the hold up?" She asked looking confused. We walked to the back. A few tears fell from Tru's eyes and I wiped them one at a time. Seeing her so emotional saddened my spirits and I began to cry as well.

"Tru, this is not it for us. I promise. We've walked the same streets because we from the same side. You my friend if nothing else and my Uncle once told me, finding a good friend is like finding a good lover. You hold on to them because everyone that's with you isn't for you nor are their motives pure." I quoted through sniffles. Tru nodded while gazing into my eyes. That alone made my button throb. It was something about the way she peered at me.

"Come on while I get my stuff so I can give you a kiss." I insisted walking to the cell. All eyes were on us like were Jay and Bey. I didn't have much to gather, just my gown and hygiene bag.

"Hurry up, Richards!" Ms. King yelled. Tru looked distraught. I wanted to break down, but I know if I would've broke, she would've done so as well. That would have made it harder to leave. Once inside, I cracked the door and ran into Tru's arms.

"I love you, Kadejah."

"I love you too, Tru." She grabbed my face with one hand and pulled me in closer. I close my eyes and kissed her like I'd never see her again. Chills crept down my spine as I moaned, swapping saliva with the chick I fell for within a matter of weeks. Our tongues danced and our lips wrestled. Tru pulled me into a hug and I could tell she didn't want to let go.

"Richards, it don't take ten minutes to grab a hygiene bag and a gown!" Ms. King hollered. I jumped back at the sound of her voice, afraid she might catch us in the act. Not wanting to depart I gave, Tru one last kiss on her forehead.

"Tru, I have to go. I'll see you later." I stated slowly backpedaling. She was downright distraught.

"Bye, Kadejah," Tru mumbled.

"Don't say bye. You only supposed to say bye when you don't plan on ever seeing someone again. I'll be seeing you real soon." I assured walking out of the cell. I quickly walked out the wing to avoid seeing Tru's face for a final time. I didn't want my family to see me teary eyed and heartbroken. Outside of the tank, Mr. Woods awaited to escort me.

"Here we go again." I mumbled.

CHAPTER 17
LIL TIM

The aroma of bacon, sausage, and something unfamiliar, yet appeasing awoke me from my slumber. Peaches had been doing a bit more than usual to get a nigga to stay out of them streets. Crazy thing is, she believed it was actually working, but it's not. The laws been hot looking for someone to pin Meeche's murder on. I figured why not chill here and lay low. Wake up and lay down to some good pussy and fire head. She stayed in that kitchen over the stove barely dressed. I couldn't ask for nothing more. She know I'm a king and she treats me as such.

"What you cooking?" I asked from the doorway of the kitchen. Peaches stood over the stove with a pink lace bra and matching boy shorts with white fluffy slippers. The site instantly made me rock up, but I tamed the beast inside of my pants 'cause I was hungry as hell. She didn't respond, although I knew she heard me.

"Aye, Peaches!"

"Huh?" She questioned dryly, instantly vexing my spirit.

"What's your problem?" I ask irritated. Nigga been shacked up with this bitch for two days straight and she still finds something to bitch about.

"I don't have a problem." She lied, handing me my plate. Blueberry waffles, bacon, sausage, cheesy scrambled eggs, and chocolate chip muffins with juice.

"Fuck what she going through." I mumbled rushing to the table to demolish my food. I picked up my fork and dug in.

"So, that's it?" She asked standing beside me with her hand on her hip.

"Is what it?" I asked with a mouth full of food.

"You not going to ask what's bothering me?" She picked.

"Say check this, holler at me when I'm done eating and if you talking nonsense, don't talk at all. Now get away from me before I drop everything and leave right now." I threatened.

She smacked her lips and strutted to the other sofa. Just when I was speaking highly of the bitch, she shows her ass. Peaches was rider and she was sexy. I just couldn't see myself giving a chick like her my all. I finished up my food and sat beside Peaches on the couch. She tried to bullshit like she was into the TV but I knew she was faking. She should've at least changed it to something other than ESPN.

"Aye." I voiced, nudging her arm.

"I just want to know one thing, Tim. Who were you up texting all night last night?"

"If you must know, I wasn't texting. I was sending Kadejah a JPay."

"It was mighty long." She added. Without responding, I hopped on my feet and raced to the bedroom.

"Tim!" She followed me through the house, but it was pointless. I retrieved my clothes from the edge of her bed and quickly got dressed. Tucking my burner in my jeans, I headed for the door.

"I hate you!" She shouted from the bedroom.

All you had to do was enjoy a niggas presence! I just don't understand female's man. Nigga break bread with you, fuck you good and I'm a street nigga. Yet, I still make time for you and it's still not enough. I can just fuck you down and burn out as soon as I pull out because you going to want the wood regardless because its superb. I give the bitch more than that and she still trip. I think I might try interracial dating cause them black bitches are unnecessary stress. I made my way down the steps. Peaches stayed eyeing me as I walked to my car. One of the niggas I spotted chilling with Peaches couple weeks ago, who she claimed was her brother. I let her think I believed her, but truth is, I just didn't care to protest.

"That's ya brother. Cool." I flashed a half smile in their direction, letting the sun beam down on the diamonds in my mouth. I hopped in my cranberry G Wagon and peeled out.

"What's up fam?" I greeted Donk, making myself comfortable on the plush sectional. Donk's home was a bit quiet, but nothing had changed.

"Look, I need to holler at you." Donk urged standing across from me while looking down at the screen on his phone. He sported a white Supreme shirt, matching jeans with a tan pair of Yeezy boots.

"What's up, fam? Rap." I stated.

"Look, I'm about to go pick up Kadejah. I need you to go check out the spot in Tyler. Make sure everything is everything and it's running smoothly." He requested.

"Kadejah coming home?" I asked in disbelief.

"Yeah, I forgot to tell you. Steve made something shake like always, but shit went down exactly how Kadejah said it did. She was merely defending herself."

"Hell yeah! What y'all got planned? I want to chill with my lil' baby, too!" I rambled off, enthused about the good news. I had missed Kadejah's little gangster ass.

"I'm going to scoop her up and take her to see Arianna then do a little shopping. Later on, we going to see that new movie by Jordan Peele called *Us* with Lupita. I think she saw the previews in there because that's all she been talking about." Donk stated, grinning from ear to ear.

"Okay, I'm going to at least try and catch the movie with y'all. If I can't, just know something came up." I stated, standing to my feet.

"Where's wifey?" I continued.

"She at that hospital." Donk replied, cutting off the lights and activating the alarm system.

"Did you take that loot by Ol' Boy's granny house?" Donk asked referring to Meech.

"Yeah, did that 'bout a week ago." I assured declining the steps.

"Look, tomorrow night, I got thirty thousand on a fight and fifteen thousand on a race." Donk informed slowing his pace.

"Nascar?" I asked in absolute shock.

"Hell nah, track and field." Donk admitted smiling

"Nigga, you getting out of control. Next you'll be betting on Serena Williams and Tiger Woods." I quipped leaning on the hood of my whip.

"Shut up. The moral of that is the white boy Kyle I introduced you to at the Buffalo Wild Wings is hosting a fight party at his place tomorrow. If you can, I want you to drop by." He stated moving toward his car.

"Okay, bet and tell Kadejah I love her!" I shouted climbing into my whip.

Me and Reggie bobbed our heads to Gunna's *Drip Season* mixtape as I sped down 635. I tried to get Bando to ride with me but he claimed the spot was booming so hard he didn't have time to piss.

I let him do his own thing. He could have easily let Lil Zane hold it down, but he refused, which told me he had some shit of his own going on. As long as the daily quotas were met, getting rid of your own pack was never an issue. I told Reggie to let Ceelo hold things down and roll with me. Peaches had been blowing my line up since this morning but I wasn't going to just give in so easily. She needed to learn how to appreciate a nigga more. Tyler was just 40 to 50 minutes away. The drive isn't what bothered me, it was the set up. Ever since my boy Q got jammed up in Midland, I try to stay from around those small ass country towns. They gave dude twenty years for a burner and three grams of Coke. I didn't bother to call Rondo and Smiley.

"Aye, word on the street, that nigga you murked had an open casket funeral." He informed. I paused, not knowing how to respond.

"I'm saying that to say, ya boy supposed to have called the cleanup crew, right?" He informed.

"Yeah." I answered dumbfounded; Reggie was speaking in riddles and I couldn't grasp the premonition.

"When the cleanup crew cleans up, they leave nothing left to identify."

Reggie climbed out of the whip. A silver Honda sat in the driveway of the spot. The house wasn't in the best condition, but definitely wasn't the worse. The lawn could use a little trimming but everything else seemed perfectly fine. Me and Reggie climbed the porch steps. I could hear *Young Jeezy* blaring through the

146

house. I used my spare key to unlock the door. I cracked it just enough to peep in and see what was occurring. Rondo was on the phone with his legs kicked up, watching the camera on the 50' plasma. Smiley was at the table breaking down the packs.

I swiftly swung the door open and both Rondo and Smiley had guns pointing our way. Smiley was a little slow getting to his, but Rondo was on point for the both of them.

"Chill, niggas!" I raised my hands in mock surrender.

"Y'all fools scared the shit out of me. I was thinking how the fuck these niggas get inside?" Rondo reckoned.

"Don't play like that." Smiley joked placing the gun on the table.

"Why you have the screen on the camera in the alley? Why all four screens aren't up?" I asked curiously

"Well, about twenty minutes ago, it was some fiends back there fighting so I zoomed in. That shit was hella funny, bruh!" Rondo explained in between laughter.

"Fuck them fiends. Niggas will use anything to distract you and get you off your A game. Hoe's ain't the only ones distracting these days." Reggie stated, standing in the center of the room while slowly monitoring things around the house.

"Hell yeah, he right." I agreed sitting down on the slightly worn out sofa. Brown bed sheets covered the windows. I guess them niggas said fuck curtains.

"Man Tim, niggas ain't going to fuck with us. They already know what it is." Smiley boasted, waving the pistol in the air.

"Check this, Donk wanted me to swing by and see how shit rolling down here, but I'm going to stay a little while longer. I'm going to just give y'all the rest of the night off. Be back around 7 AM." I instructed.

"Hell yeah! Bet." Smiley said standing to his feet, stuffing bills in one pocket and his .38 in the other.

"This the pack that was dropped off two days ago. More than half sold already and I was in the process of breaking the rest of it down into twenties and tens. I got some nicks bagged up too. I know y'all niggas done graduated from that shit, but I ain't letting

147

no money get away from me. I'll even do a few crumbs for three dollars." Smiley stated using his hand to iron out the wrinkles and wipe away and residue from his shirt.

"Fam, could you take us to pick up my car? This lil' crazy broad Rondo fuck with knocked one of his taillights out last night." He continued.

"Yeah, come on." I agreed standing to my feet.

"Pick up some cigarillos and a few Hot & Readys from Lil Ceasars. Oh, and hit the switch on them lights so I can get a better look at these cameras." Reggie hollered out from behind me while Rondo, Smiley and I took off.

CHAPTER 18
REGGIE

"Young niggas," I mumbled looking around the efficient, yet messy setting. I picked up the remote off of the table and switched it back to multiple screens. The dope that was bagged and ready I placed in my pocket and hid the rest of the dope inside a Frosted Flakes cereal box. The light from the 50-inch plasma was enough for me. As an adolescent, I was used to the dark. Momma never had the money to keep the lights or water bill paid, so eventually I became accustomed to it. As I got older, I still wasn't a big fan of lights. I liked the inside of my ride black and my tint dark.

My apartment was black everything. Curtains, furniture, carpet and bedroom set. Most of all, I wanted to experience the element of surprise. When I was younger, two dudes broke into my mother's house and took the only TV, DVD player and microwave we owned. I was just ten years of age. No peach fuzz, just a bird chest, I was no match for the goons so I tucked my tail and fled like a coward to safety under the bed. Mama said our house was targeted because they figured no one was home. Since then, I been laying low like a vampire, hoping a nigga would try me. I can guarantee you it won't be a repeat.

I propped my feet on the table while I monitored the plasma carefully. Minutes had passed and there was still no sign of Lil Tim. I rose up and headed to the kitchen to silence my growling stomach. The house was exceptionally quiet. The only noise was the faucet that dripped against the metal sink occasionally.

Knock! Knock! Knock! Moving back from kitchen, I walked toward the slide door, which was connected to the alley. I peeped through the sheet and spotted two fiends. The slide door had a metal stick at the bottom that refrained the door from opening any further than three inches; It was merely enough to make a transaction. "Brother, let me get a dime rock." The fiend requested, handing me a handful of crumbled bills. I pulled the bills apart to count them one at a time.

"1, 2, 3, 4, 5—"

"Aye, hurry up!" The fiend yelled.

"Shut the fuck up before I take yo' money and you won't get shit!" I retorted. Just as I thought he was short; two bucks shy of ten.

"Since you want to play on my intelligence, get the fuck out here and don't come back." I continued slamming the slide door shut and locking it.

"Come on man, I'm sorry. Can you at least give me my money back, please?" The cluck begged. I didn't even respond. I walked into the kitchen and peered into the fridge. Only a third of a gallon of Oak Farms milk, baking soda, a half empty 2 liter of Mountain Dew and a bottle of Hunts Ketchup. I didn't expect the fridge to have nothing more than a stick of butter in the inside. I was hoping it did, though. I headed back into the front room. The sound of a flock of footsteps approaching induced me to fall back into the shadows, pull my burner out and post up against the wall.

Boom!

The thunderous noise startled me and I tightened my finger on the burner. "All I got is seventeen shots. Please don't let it be a gang of niggas." I silently prayed.

Boom!

The door flew open and the intruders swarmed in. I peeked my head around the corner and spotted two men. One of them was flipping over the pillows on the couch. The other guy was headed my way. I opened fire.

Bock! Bock!

A bullet slammed into his chest, forcing him to stagger. The other pierced his throat. Instantly, blood squirted from his neck and he clenched his throat with both hands, but it was useless. I witnessed him drop to his knees. His man looked up in shock and began firing shots in my direction. One of the bullets whizzed past my head. I ducked low and made my way toward the opposite side of the room away from the illuminating TV. My attire made it difficult for him to hit me being that he house was so dark. Crouched down on the side of the loveseat in the far corner, I watched dude fire shots blindly. He peered around the room slowly watching and listening for any sudden movement.

Knock! Knock! Knock!

"Come on man, here's two more dollars!" The fiend yelled diverting the gunman's attention. I sprang up from the side of the loveseat and drilled him from behind, rapidly hitting him. Twice in the back and once in his skull, making his head burst like a cantaloupe. The fiend's constant knocking didn't make it any better. I tucked the burner in the waist of my jeans and headed for the front door, only to be met by the barrel of a gun. I shook my head in disbelief at the dude that stood in front of me.

"I thought I saw all you niggas leave." He stated.

"Fuck you, bitch ass nigga. I ain't kissing ass or sucking dick for a few extra seconds to live." I scolded looking him in his eyes.

"Oh you brave, huh? Just know the cautious ones get got."

He was right, I was the last nigga who'd get caught slipping. But even mouse beats the cat occasionally.

"Bitch nigga, you live to die. Nobody not excluded. Go ahead and burn me, bitch! My niggas gon' return the favor." I spat.

Bock!

Ah'Million

CHAPTER 19
LIL TIM

I pulled up to the spot and climbed out the whip. I know Lil Reggie going to be hot as fish grease 'cause I took a little longer than I intended, fucking around with them chicken heads with Rondo and Smiley's ass. Pizza in one hand, I jogged to the front door. I shoved my key into the lock surprisingly, pushing the door open.

"What the fuck?" I thought making my way inside. The gruesome sight sent chills down my spine and my eyes grew twice its normal size. The boxes of pizza hit the floor and I thought my legs would give out as I stood there awe struck at Reggie's lifeless body. Half of his face was gone and he lay motionless, gun still in hand.

"Damn fam. I should've took you with me." I thought walking over his dead body. I turned on the lights and found two more dead bodies. One of the guys I never saw a day in my life, but the other dude looked a little familiar. Even if I merely saw him briefly. At a club or casino, maybe a gas station or grocery store. I know I've seen him before.

Whoop! Whoop!

"Shit!" I cursed in terror. I didn't know if I should stay in and surrender because I'm innocent or run. If I surrender and them hoes find that dope, they going to try and give a nigga the death penalty. I could hear footsteps approaching but I didn't slow my pace.

"Police! Stop and put your hands in the air!" The cop yelled from what sounded like the entry way. I didn't even waste my time looking back. I slid the door open and flew out. The grass was as tall as a toddler, but I kept moving until I was on concrete. I looked left to right and quickly decided left. I could hear the police behind me as I made my way through the dark alley. I focused on breathing through my nostrils so I wouldn't find myself posted against a fence out of breath. I could see bright lights ahead, which was the last thing I needed, as I came to the end of the alley.

Avoiding the busy intersection, I veered to the right. Up ahead resembled a wooden area. The breathing technique didn't last long. My focus was getting the cops off my heels so I can find a nice hiding spot until tomorrow. The area consisted of high grass and large trees. What I didn't see was the small body of water I found myself knee deep in. I bolted through the water as fast as I could, but it wasn't fast enough. I looked over at the policeman who was behind me but hadn't caught up. I begin to strip out of my shirt as I made my way out of the water. I stripped down to just my black boxer briefs, in hopes of blending in with the dark skies. I could hear a dog barking in the distance, which gave me a boost in energy. My plan of nudity failed once I saw the lights on the helicopter shining down on me.

"Make it easy on yourself and just stop." The policeman spoke through the bullhorn. I could only imagine the bright light dancing on my back as I quickly moved through the woods. I was gasping for air while managing a quick and steady pace. However, I was no match for the bolts of electricity that traveled through my body. I tried to keep moving but the impact of the second hit sent me crashing onto the pavement.

CHAPTER 20
DONK

The ringing phone awoke me from a peaceful sleep. Kadejah and Arianna were home. The doctor cleared her and she was allowed to leave with us yesterday. Wifey was snuggled up under my chin, buried in my chest.

The toll free number startled me and instantly put me on the defensive. I sat up straight in my bed and clicked the switch on the lamp that sat on the nightstand.

"To accept charges, press one for other options please hold." I hit one cutting off the operator.

"You have a collect call from…Tim." My chest tightened and my suspicion was confirmed. I was hoping it was anyone other than Lil Tim.

"Yo." I picked up.

"Say fam, I'm out here in this cracker ass town on some bogus ass charges. When I say bogus, I mean bogus! I need you to call Steve and I need you to shoot down here and come see me ASAP so I can lace you up. I got booked about two hours ago. I just made it upstairs. What time is it?" He asked.

I removed the phone from my ear and looked down at the screen on my phone. "Its 5:12 AM. What time is visiting hours?"

"It's starts at 7 AM and ends at 5 PM."

"Alright, I'm about to call Steve. Get up and get dressed and I'm on my way."

"Alright."

"Bet." I stated ending the call. I lightly shook Persuasia, awakening her from her slumber.

"Hmmm." She moaned opening one eye.

"Look, Tim locked up. I'm about to go see him. He out in Tyler." I informed getting out of bed.

"Who?" She yelled, raising up.

"Lil Tim." I repeated scrolling through my contacts for Steve's number.

"You want me to come? I don't have to be at work until ten. I can go straight to work from there if need be." She insisted.

"Nah, bae, get you some sleep. I'm taking the girls."

"You sure?"

"Yes, go back to bed" I assured kissing her forehead.

"Yo, Steve." I spoke as I headed to the bathroom.

"Yeah." He whispered sluggish.

"Aye, I need you to wake up and get ready. Tim done got his self into some big trouble out in Tyler. He in Smith County. I need you to get on it and see what's going on so I can post his bond."

"Give me an hour." He assured.

"Bet." I removed my navy blue boxer briefs and hopped in the shower. The hot water flowing down my back felt like heaven. A sweet escape from everything. No later than the minute I turned the water off, I was snapped back into reality. I dressed comfortably in a pair of all black Nike joggers, a white Nike shirt that read Everyday I'm Hustling in black and money green, trimmed in gold I was wearing a pair of money green Nike Foamposites. No chain, just a Rolex and a couple sprays of Dolce & Gabanna Light Blue cologne.

"Kadejah, baby girl, wake up."

"Huh, Unc?"

"Get dressed. You and Arianna. We about to go see Lil Tim."

"Where he at?" She questioned.

"Just get dressed. I'll let you know once we get in the car."

"Okay." She responded pulling the covers back. Kadejah had really grew, if only Quaylo could see her now. I know Rochelle would have her spoiled rotten. She had Quaylo swag and her attitude. I warmed up a couple Jimmy Dean's breakfast bowls for me and the kids. It was now ten pass six.

"Y'all ready?" I asked standing in the center of the kitchen.

***

The jail setting resembled an old 1960's hospital. Something straight out of a horror film. From the décor to the weird looking officers. It was so bad that I contemplated on telling Kadejah and Arianna to sit in the car.

"I'm here to visit Timothy Fulton." I stated, standing in front of the counter while hand in hand with Arianna and Kadejah. The ugly, thin haired white guy continued to chew the tobacco. His teeth were brown and shaped like crystals, the few he had left. He resembled one of the characters from the horror movie, *The Hills Have Eyes.*

"Wait over there, he'll be out in a minute. The waiting area consist of a payphone and one wooden chair. Minutes had passed and I was becoming impatient, but these crackers were so dirty. I'll probably be somewhere swimming with the fishes.

"Unc, I'm going to sit down." Kahdejah stated before sitting in the chair.

'Yeah, let Arianna sit in your lap." I added, posted against the wall. Although Arianna and Kadejah were the same age, Arianna was much smaller. Two inches shorter and about 20 pounds lighter. She hadn't uttered a word since the day I picked her up. Kadejah had become hysterical when I informed her on PJ's situation but thanks to Steve, he was also awaiting his release.

"Follow me." A red haired, ill built woman stated leading the way. We walked down the off white vestibule, which was short and narrow. She opened a door to the left where Lil Tim sat behind the Plexiglass. The room was exceedingly small. I let the girls sit on the ledge while I remained standing.

"You got forty five minutes." She announced closing the door. Lil Tim eyes grew wide with excitement seeing Kadejah. However, the look she returned was full of grief and fear. I picked up the phone from the wall but Tim motioned for me to stop.

"I'm going to talk to you without the phone cause it's recording." He voiced loudly.

"Aye, y'all sit on this stool." I stated, helping Arianna off the ledge. I need to be as close to the glass as possible so I wouldn't miss a beat.

"Alright, start from the top." Lil Tim informed me on everything that happened from the time he picked up Reggie.

"What? You saw what?" I interrupted his story.

"Reggie was laid out with half of his face blown off. Some niggas had ran in on him while I was gone. It was two dead bodies with his."

"Hold up, hold up, man. You telling me Reggie dead, Tim? I asked deliriously. I begin grinding my teeth to compose the anger that fumed inside of me. I allowed Tim to finish his story. Visualizing Reggie's lifeless body diverted my focus from time to time. I'd grown used to having Reggie around. He reminded me of Mun in so many ways. He knew the dope game like he invented it and could decipher the real from the fake with ease. Reggie wasn't the type to get caught slipping. According to Lil Tim's version of the story, it didn't sound like he was slipping. Just merely out numbered.

"So, what they trying to charge you with?" I asked a bit exasperated.

"Three capital murders and a manufacturing and delivering charge."

"Fuck!" I yelled hitting the glass with my fist. If it wasn't one thing, it was another.

"Chill, Donk, they can't put them murders on me, man. I didn't do that shit!" Lil Tim cried out.

"Man, you right. I'm just so fucked up about Reggie ass and to now hear this. I'm all fucked up." I responded. Lil Tim's head fell into the palm of his hands.

"Aye, lil nigga, pick your head up. You pay a price to suit up on the front line. That's how it is when you choose this life. We gon' mourn lil' bro and keep it pushing. We don't have no choice. You not going to be here no longer than three days. The murders not going to stick and soon as they give you a bond I'm going to post it." I assured.

Tim nodded his head in agreement while he motioned for Kadejah to pick up the phone. I couldn't make out what they were saying and wasn't trying to. I was so mesmerized in my own thoughts. Losing one of my best soldiers wasn't a pleasant feeling, but this sounded like an inside job to me. It was time for me to put my Tom Ford loafers up and lace up my 95's and fade the streets again.

"Times up." The red head yelled, propping the door open.

"Alright family, I love you boy." I stated chunking the deuce. Before heading back to Dallas, I rolled past the spot. Yellow caution tape surrounded the house and I just shook my head remembering the loss I took. Yeah the cash would hurt my pockets a little but Reggie? My dawg. I don't even know how I was going to tell his mother. I was about to pull off when I spotted a fiend walking in my direction, mumbling something underneath his breath.

"Aye , man, come here!" I yelled as I motioned him toward the car. He looked around skeptically before marching my way.

"Brother, tell him I got the two dollars." He rambled on

"What?"

"I…I gave him eight, but I got the two. I got it. It's right here" He stuttered.

"What are you talking about? Who is him?" I inquired.

"The brother in that house from last night." He pointed.

"Did you see what happened last night?"

"Maybe." He said looking from my eyes to my Rolex.

"Here, take this and tell me everything." I stated peeling off a twenty dollar bill.

"Some guys ran in the house so I didn't try to get my dope cause I heard gunshots. Then, it stopped so I start knocking. Then, I heard more gunshots. So I took off. Well, soon I hit the corner on my way back around and I see this big guy walk in. I kept it moving and by the time I get a few houses down, I hear one gunshot. I looked back and saw dude peel off.

"What kind of car was dude in? I snooped through squinted eyes.

"Uh.. *o tjoml ot wa s a, gmi, pr a cjarger.* It was all black." He added scratching his armpits.

"Tell me one more time how dude looked." I prodded.

"Well, brother, it was mighty dark. But I would say he was probably bout 6'2 close to 280 pounds. Maybe brown skinned; not too dark but a little darker than a brown paper sack." The fiend described.

"Okay, bet." The description didn't sound too familiar, but maybe someone will come to mind once I settle down.

"Brother, you know where I can get some good at?" He asked rubber necking.

"Yeah, come on." I replied climbing out the whip.

"I'll be right back, don't move." I whispered to Kadejah. I led the junky toward the house, but veered off to the side, which led to the back. The sliding door was up ahead. I swiftly turned on my heels.

Psst!

The silenced gun went off.

"Aarrggghh!" The junky yelped out in pain while gripping his shoulder.

"Why you shoot me man?" He cried staggering over the empty beer cans. I slowly walked towards the fiend, strap in hand.

"Because nigga you should've helped my dawg, but yo' cracked out ass was trying to get a fix."

"How was I 'pose to help, man?" He plead gripping his shoulder with tears in his eyes.

"Hell if I know. You should've died trying." I sent a bullet in between his eyes, silencing him forever, and then I hit the corner before his body hit the floor.

***

"Is she talking yet?" I asked Kadejah who sat comfortably on the sofa watching the repeat episodes of Claws. Although Kadejah seem enthused to be home, there were many times she acted a bit despondent.

"Nope." She nonchalantly responded never taking her eyes off the T.V.

"Little girl, what's been going on with you? What's with the long face?" I asked.

"Well, Unc. You know I've always been honest with you because you don't judge me." She stated. "When I was in juvenile those few weeks, I met this girl that I grew attached to, and being away from her shows me just how much I miss and truly love her." She admitted. I shook my head and began reminiscing about Quaylo's gay ass. *At least it's not one of those little roughish ass niggas*, I thought.

"Look, I'm not for that gay shit. Although, I'm not against it either. If she make you happy, do you. I just don't want to talk about it or entertain the idea, baby girl. Talk to P. Maybe she can relate." I expressed trying not to sound so harsh.

"But, Unc. Persuasia isn't never home anymore." She whined.

"Yeah, that hospital kicking her ass" I shot back sitting next to her on the sofa.

"If you say so." She mumbled.

"What you doing over there on that phone that has so much of your attention?" I asked ignoring her fly comment.

"I'm adding funds to Lil Tim's commissary account and dropping him a few lines with a few selfies."

"Where you get some money from?" I inquired half joking.

"My allowance, duh, Uncle Donk. Speaking of that, can you add more money to my cards?"

"I got you. Tell Lil Tim that I love him, and Steve is on top of it."

"Okay." She responded.

"Look, I'm about to head out. I got to be in the mix a little more since Reggie gone, but if you need anything, just call me. If you leave, let me know where you at. And if you in danger..."

"The .380 under the wood in the fireplace." Kadejah mocked, finishing my sentence. "I know Unc, I know." She continued with a smile.

"Here, take this until I add to your card." I insisted placing two crisp hundred dollar bills in her palm.

"I love you, Unc." She expressed.

"I love you too." I shot back placing a kiss on her forehead. I walked into PJ's room and peeked in on Arianna before leaving the house.

I hadn't spoken to Mya much since our last little hook up. I was planning on pulling up on her and returning her phone calls once everything was situated. I informed Rondo and Smiley on the new location they'll be setting up at in a few days. I swung by Reggie's mother's place a little white ago to check on her and give her a couple stacks to ensure Reggie receives the proper burial. I was told that the cops informed her about his death the following morning. I gave her my condolences and we talked for a few minutes before I left. Without announcing my presence, I unlocked the door to the spot on Fish Trap Rd.

"Ceelo!" I called out, who I spotted sitting across the room at a circular wooden table, clutching a bottle of E&J

"Damn, Donk, I didn't even know that was you!" He yelled leaping to his feet. His eyes were red and glossy and I could tell by his tear stained cheeks that he'd been crying. T. Grizzly's lyrics played at a moderate volume. My mama locked up/ Lil bro still locked up/ my daddy got popped up/ and now I'm fucked up.

Suddenly, I felt sympathetic as I thought about him and Reggie's bond.

"You alright?" I asked looking around the place. Pizza boxes were stacked on the coffee table and the garbage can was full to its capacity. Clothes were strewn across the foot along with other miscellaneous items.

"Yeah I'm good." Ceelo responded rubbing his face to remove any proof that he'd been crying, moving around the house quickly rearranging things.

Knock! Knock!

"I got it, get yourself together." I stated looking out the peephole.

"Give me a dub." The fiend commanded as soon as I opened the wooden door. Ceelo handed me the pack and I made the transaction through the burglar bars. I sat on the old but snug sofa while Ceelo fixed things up.

"Aye, until I find someone to replace Reggie I'm going to be in and out. If something comes up and you need me to hold it down, just hit me up, but for the most part, I'll be here." I informed.

Knock! Knock!

"I got this one, big homie." Ceelo insisted. I didn't know a lot about Ceelo but I fucked with him off the strength of Reggie. I knew if Reggie said he was good, then that's all that mattered. Tonight was the night of the fight and I couldn't wait to collet. Since Tim was locked up, I decided to just go alone, which was fine with me. The race should be starting momentarily, but with everything going on, I'll have to skip that and catch the highlights so I can collect as well. I let Ceelo leave for a few hours while I held things down. Shit was pretty smooth. The whole setup. Reggie had changed a few things around, but it was for the better. Lord knows I was going to truly miss my nigga. Ceelo returned with a new fit, new cut looking like new money.

"You good?" I smiled, enthused to see him in good spirits.

"Yeah fam, 'preciate ya for everything."

"You good. Just keep ya head up, lil' nigga. You going to take losses in more ways than one, but all you can do is stand tall. It's designed to break you but allow it to build you and you'll be good." I quoted looking at a teary eyed Ceelo. He quickly blinked them away before they fell, nodding in approval.

Before I could even ask Persuasia to accompany me to the party, she informed me about a friend from work's bachelorette party she'd be attending. I didn't even bother throwing the idea out there to put her in a situation where she would have to choose. It wasn't too serious. Mya crossed my mind, but I decided against the idea as well. I swung by the house to retrieve the 30K. The party started in ten minutes and Kyle stayed a pretty nice distance away from me. Kadejah and Arianna were in the kitchen eating cereal when I walked in.

"Y'all good?" I asked breathing heavy.

"Yes, Unc. Where you been?" Kadejah called out from the kitchen

"None of your business." I joked over my shoulder as I hurried to the stash inside of my bedroom. I could tell Persuasia had come and left because her Coco Mademoiselle Chanel perfume lingered. I stuffed the stacks in a Nike shopping bag and fixed everything back the way it was.

"Persuasia been here?" I asked knowing the answer.

"Yeah her and Esha left about ten minutes ago." She responded.

"Esha?" I asked curiously. I thought she was attending a friend at work party."

"Yeah, Esha. She had her Louis Vuitton duffel bag in her hand." She squealed.

"Oh okay." I stated shrugging off the situation with Persuasia. I looked over at a quiet Arianna, who was staring back at me.

Man, I just wish she would say something, anything. I thought. I went and kissed both girls on the forehead and left.

"Donk! My man!" Kyle yelled holding his arm out for a hug. I politely stuck my hand out allowing him to shake it. I could tell dude was taken back by gesture. He grabbed my hand with the both of his and shook it vigorously. I excused his debauched behavior and made my way into the plush foyer. A bartender was to the left serving behind the bar. A 72 inch plasma decorated the spacious room. It was about twenty to thirty people present. Some dressed for the occasion and a few overly dressed. Maybe I wasn't dressed for the occasion. I still had the same gear on that I had on earlier. The bitches didn't seem to trip as I noticed the several stares and winks I got from different women, even the women who were with their man or husband.

Bitches were so sneaky. I'm glad I chose the chick I got because she wasn't with the fuckery. Seven years we've been thugging, going long and strong. The only reason I hadn't proposed is because I believe in signs. Eights my lucky number, so in a few weeks from now when we get to the big eight, I'm going to gladly fall to one knee. I already purchased the 10-carat ring almost a year ago.

I continued to admire Kyle's lavish crib. The interior design was dope. The dope chocolate brown walls matched the brown and auburn furniture. Massive floor to ceiling windows adorned the walls. I was impressed. The front room was set up like a restaurant almost. Circle wood grain tables scattered around the spacious front room. Kyle had a spot reserved for us on the sectional, which was closer to the TV than the tables. Waitresses walked around and took beverage orders while passing out the menu. A lot of the stuff on the menu was too fancy to my liking. I wasn't appeased at all by the difficult names. I'm a regular ol' hood nigga. The only thing I was familiar with was the lemon peppered wings.

"Would you like to order, sir?" The amiable waitress asked. She was about twenty pounds under weight. And her teeth looked false. Her blonde hair was stringy, but she had a nice personality.

"Yeah, let me have ten of those lemon peppered wings." I requested closing the menu and handing it to her.

"Okay, I'll be right back." She winked before walking way. I chuckled at her boldness. I just hope she don't try and take it any further.

"You like it, buddy?" Kyle asked sitting in the loveseat that was positioned between the two couches.

"Hell yeah, it's nice." I complimented sipping on my Hen.

"Yeah, I got three of the finest dancers money can buy after the fight ends." He boasted crossing his legs.

"Okay, cool!" I'll have plenty of money to throw." I bragged.

"We'll see about that." He stated. The bell sounded, indicating the fight had begun.

"I'm Mandy. Call me when you're done." She insisted, handing me a tray of seasoned and delicious looking wings.

"Marquez about to give Jones ass the business." I boasted in between bites. The lemon peppered wings were as delicious as they looked. Kyle's guest wasn't what I expected. I was looking for people that looked and acted like Kyle. Instead, it was many men of my color with expensive suits who possessed business savvy. They're chicks were on point as well. The few that

165

resembled Kyle wore suits as well, but obviously money can't buy loyalty because they're women gawked at me like I was an ass naked statue.

"These hoes act like they have never seen or been around a real nigga before." I thought licking the sauce off the tip of my thumb.

"We'll see about that, but you can give me fifteen thousand. According to ESPN, my girl won." He boasted winking his eye.

"I'm about to go see for myself, and if that's the case, I don't mind paying what I owe. "I stated retrieving my phone from my pocket.

"Oooohhh!" The crowd erupted, entailing me to divert my attention from my phone. I missed the blow that had the crowd damn near on their feet. I knew once the round ended they would replay it. Both men moved swiftly to avoid one another's blows. Jones threw a quick left Marquez ducked the left and counter punched a right hook to his temple making Jones' jaw jerk. With tight lips, I grinned at Kyle, who acted unbothered by the blow. He never moved his eyes from the screen until the bell sounded, indicating round one was over. I quickly scrolled down the ESPN app and it was clear as day the winner of the race. I had the 15K separate from the 30K that I stored into the Nike bag. I retrieved the stack of money that I had placed in my pocket before handing it to Kyle.

"'Preciate ya." He mocked.

"Mandy." I called out ignoring Kyle's comment. She looked in my direction and hurried towards me.

"You're finished?" She asked, taking the empty plate from my hand.

"Anything else?" She continued.

"Just a refill." I stated handing her the empty glass of Hennessey. Round two started and the men went at it like women do in a cat fight. I smiled as I recanted a few girl fights from my days. They didn't bob, weave, duck, move or dance. They just ran into one another and start swinging. I remember my mother's first lessons to my older sister, Quaylo. One day Quaylo had come home from school with a knot on her forehead. According to that knot, she used more than her fist. Quaylo explained the fight she just had inside of the girl's restroom.

"You telling me she got the best of you?" My mom asked. "Quaylo?" My momma asked rhetorically. She knew the answer once Quaylo remained tight-lipped. "Do she got a knot or a busted lip?" My mother continued.

"No ma'am, it was hard for me to hit her." Quaylo responded with her head hung low.

"Let me tell you something." Mama stated squatting down positioning herself face to face with Quaylo.

"Ninety five percent of women, especially ones your age don't fight strategically. They get themselves roused up and dive in headfirst. You windmill. You know what I mean by windmill?" My mother demonstrated. "Head up and windmill you a bitch. I guarantee you'll land something. She going to know you was there. I can bet you that. Watch what I tell you."

My thoughts drifted back to the TV screen. The men grew tired. Round six was underway and still nothing had happened the deter the best contender. I watched on diligently. The realization of the 15K loss settled in and I was determined to win that back plus some. Marquez hit Jones with an uppercut that sent him flying backwards to the ropes, but Jones maneuvered out of the corner that he was nearly forced in.

"Fuck! Quez, you should've cleaned his ass up!" I yelled as I reclined on the couch. I glanced over at Kyle, who was studying the fight like the TV was the professor and he was the student. An unexpected two piece sent Marquez down. He had been on top the majority of the fight. Now, he was seconds away from the first loss of his career.

"Seven, eight, nine, ten." The referee and the crowd counted aloud along with Kyle. Kyle peered over at me with a cunning smile.

"Today was ya lucky day." I commented proudly handing over the Nike shopping bag. "I would love to stay and mingle, but now I go to shake back my boy." I said shaking Kyle's hand. I was mad than a motherfucker but I refused to show it. A thick Puerto Rican chick walked out with a duffle bag in her hand. She wore a red strapless dress that barely covered her juicy ass cheeks. She sat the bag down, removed the pole and begin to set it up.

"You not staying for the show?" Kyle asked.

"Nah nigga, you got all my money." I quipped. I will take a cup of Hen to go." I continued scanning the crowd for Mandy.

"Oh, that's cool. You want something to eat too?"

"Nah, I'm cool on the wings. Tell Mandy to bring me a bottle!" I requested.

"Mandy!" Kyle called out, snapping his finger. Mandy hurried our way. "Bring me that bottle of Hennessey, a Styrofoam cup of ice and twenty of those lemon peppered wings to go." Kyle ordered.

"Yes, sir" She stated before walking off.

"I told you I didn't want no more wings, bruh." I calmly stated.

"Yeah I know, it's not for you. It's for those little girls of yours you're always talking about." He responded.

"Oh, 'preciate ya. Nice looking out." I applauded

Megan Thee Stallion's *Big Freak* blasted through Kyle's massive house. The Puerto Rican mommy came back out. This time she was nearly nude in her dance attire. Shorty was gorgeous, but I wasn't the type of nigga to let my dick dictate the way I move. Mandy came right on time with my shit.

"Thanks, Mandy," I stated.

"Anytime." She winked handing me the white container and bottle before sashaying away. Mandy didn't have a glimpse of ass.

"Alright, Kyle!" I yelled walking towards the front door.

"What the fuck?" I mouthed scowling at a nearly nude Persuasia. She was so occupied texting a way on her phone that she hadn't looked up from her screen. Bypassing me, she went inside the area I'd just left where the party was taking place. I slowly followed her back inside when my cell phone vibrated in my pocket

Persuasia: I'll be home in a few hours daddy. I love you

I shook my head at the text. After all these years, I would've never thought Persuasia would betray me in this kind of way. To strip? Really? I give her whatever I think she wants. I chuckled to myself as I tried my best to suppress my anger. I stood behind the crowd as they gathered around to watch Persuasia pole dance and twerk her ass. I peered at Persuasia intensely through squinted eyes.

A zooted Esha walked in and Persuasia disappeared. I walked discreetly through the crowd in the direction Persuasia headed to. I locked eyes with a dumbfounded Kyle but didn't utter a word. I walked through the door down the hallway. There were doors on each side. I opened them one at a time and peeked in. The first door on the left looked like a guest room. It was empty. I peeked in the second door and there stood a naked Persuasia changing into a different outfit. She didn't even hear me walk in. Her long hair fell loosely and hung right above the crack of her ass. My first thought was to walk up behind the bitch and strangle her ass to death for playing me, but that wasn't even my steelo. A grown bitch is free to make her own decisions. If this what she want, cool beans. I shouldn't have to monitor a bitch 24/7 for her to do the right things. Sensing someone behind her, she swiftly turned on her heels.

"Oh my God! Donk, what you doing here?" She stuttered.

"Look, just get your shit and let's go!" I demanded.

"I can explain." She rambled stuffing her belonging into the Louis Vuitton duffel bag.

"I'll be waiting outside in the car." I stated walking out of the room. I bypassed Kyle again I chunked him the deuces and kept it moving. Persuasia beat me to my own car. I climbed in and pulled off.

"Donk? Bae, can I explain?" She asked. I didn't even bother to respond before she began to ramble off. The whole ride back I never uttered one word. After growing tired of hearing her, I turned the volume up on my radio to full blast to drown out her annoying voice. Slinging snot and full of tears, Persuasia walked directly beside me to further explain.

"Shhh, these kids might be asleep."

Once the door was closed to our bedroom, Persuasia broke down.

"Check this, stop crying. I'm not moved by it and cut the lies because when I was willing to listen to the truth, you lied. So, shut the fuck up. We done. The only reason I gave you a ride is because I figured the quicker you get here, the quicker you can pack and leave. You got a hour. If it take you longer than that, I'm going to help you." I stated turning on my heels.

"Donk, after all we've been through? I can't get a second chance?" She begged.

"Two is too many. One was enough," I stated before closing the door shut.

***

I watched from a distance as Kadejah, Arianna and PJ embraced one another. It brought a smile to my face to see PJ finally home. Steve had pulled it off, yet again The only thing bothering me was the possibility of him and Kadejah being split up. Blood couldn't make them any closer and through the years, they've grown to love, protect and treat each other as siblings. I hated the fact I possessed more pride than anything. My mother always told me my pride would be my downfall, if not the death of me. My pride was greater than the love I retained for PJ. There was no way I could take Persuasia back. All a nigga ask for is loyalty, assurance and sex. That's it. To go back to the old lifestyle had to mean two things. She was bored and missed that life, or she was downright delusional and I can't trust a psych patient. A delusional mothafucker. You just never know when they about to have an episode. If she take my lil nigga away, it's cool. He'll be 18 in five years and then he can decide where he wants to go. Now what's going to hurt me is if Kadejah is affected.

"What's up, lil man, you good?" I asked PJ as I brushed my hand across his nappy hair.

"Yeah I'm good, I'm free. I'm so glad to be home with y'all. Where my momma at?" He asked standing on the tip of his toes peering my through my black Denali truck. Suddenly, Kadejah chuckles cease and Arianna smile faded.

"Come on, I'll tell you all about it on the ride home."

Ah'Million

CHAPTER 21
PJ

Hearing what transpired between Donk and my mom disgruntled my spirit. As I peered out the window of Donk's truck, I sat in deep thought, hoping everything would soon be the same if not better. A part of me wanted to blame Donk, but in all aspects, he was right. However, right or wrong, that's my mother and I see no wrong in her. Over the time, I'd grown to love Donk like a father. A father I never had. He was supportive in every way possible. He attended every pee wee football game; he was like the second coach and had my back when I had my first girl. I know my mother has her side of the story as well, but what she did was total disrespect. After Donk dropped the bomb on me, it felt as if a hefty load had been placed on my shoulders.

"Don't cry, PJ." Arianna spoke in a low tone.

Skkkrrr!

The sound of screeching tires sang as Donk slammed his foot on the brakes forcing everyone bodies to jerk forward. I guess Donk was more surprised at hearing Arianna's voice. Arianna looked around sheepishly.

"When did you start talking, Arianna?" Donk asked in shock.

"Yeah Arianna, I been trying to get you to laugh, sing, hum. Anything," said Kadjeah.

"I'm sorry y'all. I tried but I always came up empty." Arianna stated, shrugging her shoulders. "The words would be formed in my head, but nothing would come out." She continued, looking up at me with those bedroom eyes.

"Maybe, she just wanted to talk to me." PJ quipped breaking the awkward silence. Kadejah rolled her eyes while Donk smirked proceeding on to his destination.

"Kadejah, let me see your phone." I said. Despite the strife between my mother and Donk, I missed her dearly and needed to see her.

"Ma, I'm home. I'll be at Donk's in a few," I said.

"I'm on my way." She responded enthused. I hung up the phone while me Arianana and Kadejah laughed and joked until we pulled up to the house. My mother's car was parked in the driveway. My heart began to beat rapidly as I climbed out of the truck. I jogged to my mother and squeezed her tight. She wore a Micheal Kors polyester jumpsuit with Christian Louboutin satin wrapped 4-inch heels. A little over the top for a Welcome Home. I squeezed her tighter, wishing we could enter our home as one big happy family again. However, this wasn't a love story with a fairytale ending. This shit was real. Donk casually strolled past us speaking into his phone, while Kadejah and Arianna conversed with my mother.

"Donk?" She called out. Donk spun around to acknowledger her.

"What's up?"

"Can I come in and spend some time with PJ?"

"Of course, come on." He stated waving us in. I retrieved sodas from the fridge for me and momma while we sat on the sofa and talked about everything. From my juvie experience, future plans and her side of the story, which turned the conversation into a ball of emotions. Tears streamed down her face and I stood to my feet to wipe her eyes with that back of my hand.

"Ma, it's going to be okay, you messed up. It's on you to make it right." I commented resting my hand on her shoulder.

"PJ, someone name Fernando wants you." Kadejah said looking dumbfounded.

"Oh shit, what up boy?" I asked enthused.

"Chilling. You free? I'm chilling with my moms right now. My papa is on his way into town. We're having a big party. If you can, I want you to slide through.

"Oh bet, I'll hit you up in a few." I said ending the call. I handed Kadejah her phone before sitting down on the couch. I told my mother I would like to stay with Donk and visit her on the weekends. She didn't bicker nor dispute about my decision.

"I'm going to go now, baby. I do have to work now." She stated putting emphasis on have.

"Not for long, mama." I shot back with a wink.

"Don't be doing anything crazy. You have two parents that gives you the world. You don't have to do nothing. Be a kid for as long as you can." She spoke drying her eyes.

"Alright, mama." I started waking her towards the door.

"Bye y'all." She hollered down the hallway, in hopes for Donk to show his face.

"Bye, Persuasia. I love you." Kadejah shot back, running into my mother's arms.

"Bye, Ms. Persuasia." Arianna stated. My mother looked at her amazed

"Oh, I forgot to tell you, Arianna can talk." I flashed a boyish grin.

My mother hugged Arianna, placing a kiss on her forehead. "I'm so happy for you, baby girl. Y'all stay out of trouble. I'll see y'all later." She voiced, rubber necking down the vestibule area toward Donk's room before walking out.

***

"Aye, pop, this my boy I was locked up with that I was telling you about." Fernando introduced.

"I'm PJ." I added offering my hand.

"Nesto, nice to meet you, PJ. We'll talk more once things simmer down." He shook my hand.

I watched Fernando's family drink beer and bop to the throw-back Southside music. At times, they'll switch it up a bit and play the salsa shit for the freaks that were in attendance. Today was a bit different. Everyone was awaiting the arrival of Fernando's grandfather. You would've thought dude was the Godfather or some shit. Supposedly, he would be in town a few weeks to check out a few business ventures to legalize more of his dirty money. Fernando had been the only person I'd hung out with since my release. I realized the friends I had before juvie just weren't on my level mentally so I pulled back.

"How old are you, papi?" A beautiful Spanish woman asked. She looked to be in her early twenties. She was slim, nice breast, no ass but a little hips with long curly hair and a beautiful thick accent.

"I'm old enough." I paused. She discreetly tossed her hair back and smiled, but before she could speak, I quickly interceded. "To be your son." She leaped up like someone had poured ice down her shirt. Those were my intentions.

I knew I was on the rise, and I refused to allow females to distract me. Persuasia, Kadejah, and Arianna were enough. Donk always told me don't be so quick to submit to a woman and don't entertain them when something more imperative is at hand. If she ain't wifey, always put her second and if for some reason up can't put her second, make her feel like she is. I wanted to stay focus on meeting Fernando's grandfather. Nesto was the man but pops was the plug.

"Fam." Fernando called out from behind.

"Yeah." I answered turning around to see him holding up a beer in his hand.

"You good?" He asked.

"Yeah, but let me holler at you." He sat the beer back into the cooler and staggered towards me.

"What's up?" He slurred plopping down into the seat next to me.

"Aye, you got some more those X pills on you?"

"Yeah, I have about ten left." He stated retrieving the bag of multicolored pills from his pocket.

"This little chick want some later. I'm just going to get them for her now." I stated handing him the sixty dollars.

"Bet." I went to stuff the pills in my pocket, but something about the pills were a little off. I poured the pills into my hand and counted out twenty pills.

"Aye fam, you slipping. This twenty pills here." I started removing my ten pills and passing him the bag back.

"Damn fool, you a real nigga. Since I been old enough to comprehend, walk and talk, my friends, even family have always tried to get over on me. You honest and it means a lot to me."

"That's petty." I shot back.

"It is but motherfuckas greedy. They want it all."

"Oooohhh, shit! Juanito!" Someone yelled out. I snapped my head in the direction of the commotion, immediately spotting the black Cadillac Escalade. A Hispanic bald guy hopped out first. He was the driver. He had an ugly scar on the side of his face and his large build was quite intimidating. He looked to be about 250lbs, standing at a little over 6'6. A black guy came from around the opposite side while the driver went and opened the door to the backseat, which I assumed was Juanito. The black guy looked a bit out of place compared to Juanito and the driver. The way I mentally imagined Juanito was totally different than the way he actually looked. He looked younger and cut. He was dressed in a multicolored Louis Vuitton, Hawaii style shirt, white cargo shorts, a pair of light brown Macri loafers and a pair of Dolce and Gabbana square sunglasses.

He didn't act snobbish or too good. He greeted every man with a rare kind of attentiveness engaging in a brief conversation before moving to the next. His long sleek ponytail was braided into one braid, which hung to the middle of his back. His salt and pepper goatee was trimmed to perfection, He kind of resembled Ice-T, the Hispanic version. Only difference is he had one gold tooth. Him and Nesto embraced the longest and I saw him whisper something in Nesto's ear. Fernando stood in line as well. It was as if it was an imaginary red carpet underneath his feet. I guess my black ass stood out like a sore thumb, because as soon as Juanito embraced Fernado, he looked into my direction, voicing something to Fernando while pointing at me. I quickly stood to my feet and made my way to Juanito trying my best to look confident.

"How you doing sir, I'm PJ." I stated holding out my hand. He stared at me for what felt like minutes before responding. Finally, he firmly shook my hand.

"I hear you're a good friend of my grandson, but I'm not easily convinced, PJ." He stated while walking away. I remained
stagnant for a few second before retreating back to my seat. I sat in
deep thought replaying Juanito's words when I looked up and saw
Juanito's bodyguard peering at me. He had more swag than
Juanito. What caught my eye was the confidence in his Gucci
tropical print lined pants. He slowly tagged behind Juanito
watching every gesture as well as the movement across the street
and everything that wasn't a part of the commotion. I don't know
if he was glancing at me continuously because I looked suspect, or
if he felt some sort of connection cause I was the only other black
in attendance.

CHAPTER 22
PERSUASIA

The past few days had been a blur. When I was sober, I would constantly beat myself up throughout the day. Listening to a bitch with no nigga, helped sway me into doing some shit to lose mine. Never trust a single bitch. Ninety percent of them single for a reason. I couldn't blame everything solely on Esha because she didn't put a gun to my head. Hell, she should've. Then, pulled the trigger. The thrill of sneaking only made it easier for me to get to dance with Esha the second time. I brought this shit upon myself. The perfect home, man and all of the above gone because I couldn't leave my past life buried. That's part of the reason I lay in this plush condo next to one of Donk's associates. Only thing is I was catfished. See dudes quick to say a bitch got over them because that night she looked like Bey but woke up looking like Jay once all her makeup was removed. At least, she can always convert back to that chick that had you mesmerized with a few beauty products. However, as women we're fucked. You have all this money, you dripping like a broke faucet, impeccable swag and arrogant as they come so a bitch put on her choosing shoes assuming if all fails, she'll at least get some good dick. You strip out of your clothes with a body like NBA star Kawhi Leonard. I just know you about to punish my ass with the pipe of my life. "No good!" As soon as the tip connect with the opening, you look down and get an instant attitude. Dude wasn't even six inches. The only reason I spent a night is because he promised to give me shopping money if I stayed the night.

"I have to get ready for work in a few hours." I stated waking his fine ass up. I was still messed up about the lame ass sex, but I had to play it off.

What a waste. I thought to myself as I eyed the small budge in his briefs.

"You want some more?" He smiled following my eyes.

"Boy, if we start we not going to be able to stop and I have to get ready for work." I lied rolling out of the bed. He looked me up and down admiring every body part. "Come on now." I giggled as I slowly began to get dressed.

"Alright, five minutes." He assured standing to his feet while proceeding to the restroom, kicking out his left leg to fix his piece inside his briefs.

Shit like that? You doing all that like you working with a monster. I thought rolling my eyes before turning my head.

"Where the fuck is my underwear?" I mouthed nearly frustrated. I massaged my temples while I slowly walk around the room in search of my Victoria Secret laced boy shorts. I looked under the pillows and under the bed but no sign of my panties.

"Fuck!" I mumbled. Fuck it, I'm just going to have to do without. I walked to the other side of the bed and grabbed my leggings. On the way down, I noticed a red lace material poking out of the closed dresser drawer. Immediately, I pulled it open revealing a draw full of panties. Each panty had a yellow sticky note with the chick's name or description attached to it.

"What the fuck?" I thought. I hurried and grabbed my panties, removing the sticky note and hiding them in my bra.

"What the hell is his weird ass up to?" I thought. I was awe struck at the absurd sight. The sound of the toilet flushing knocked me out of my trance and I quickly put on my panties before the leggings. I didn't want him to know at that moment I discovered his guilty pleasure. Able to feel the print of my panties; I went in panic mode knowing it was a possibility he would notice them and realize I'd been in his stash. Lord knows what he'll do to me for snooping. I would've never thought a dude of his caliber would possess some weird ass fetish.

"You ready?" He asked coming from the bathroom.

"Almost." I responded quickly bypassing him and locking myself inside the bathroom. I quickly stripped out of the leggings and removed my panties stuffing them between my legs. I slid my leggings back on and used the cold water from the faucet to clean my face. I rolled off a nice amount of tissue and dabbed my face until it was dry before exiting the restroom. I peeked in on him. It was evident he'd been looking for something.

"I'm ready." I stated. He secretly looked at me then to the dresser while tucking his car keys in his pocket.

"Come on." He said motioning me to go ahead of him just as I predicted he would. I know he was watching my ass trying to see if I was wearing my underwear, but I was two steps ahead.

Ah'Million

CHAPTER 23
PJ

The next morning, I hit Bando up. Now, he was game with us being business partners. All I had to do now was get the product. Me and Fernando decided to chill on the porch and play basketball when I spotted Nesto pulling up.

"What's up, Pops?" Fernando greeted.

"What's up? Just the person I wanted to see. So, PJ tells me you can sell water to a fish."

I kind of felt bad for lying, but now with Bando, I could get rid of whatever he had.

"You got some loot, lil nigga? He asked sipping on a Corona.

"I got enough to cop a cookie." I stated knowingly.

"A cookie?" He smiled at the confidence in my response.

"Shit, they come in all different shapes and sizes so the prices vary. How much you working with?" He asked.

Pulling out my entire savings that I managed to save over the years, I handed Nesto the neatly folded $600. He counted the bills while turning his lips downward, mimicking Al Pacino in the movie Scarface.

"Okay, this is a start. I got you. You know what, youngin. I can see the ambition in your eyes. I got a deal you might like." He suggested.

"If you can sell this cookie in two days, I'm going to chunk you 2 kilos. They 16.5 a pop. I want double the price plus a little extra and you can keep the rest of the profit. If you know what you doing, this will be a nice come up." I shifted from my left leg to my right, unsure of how to respond. I didn't want to accept any favors without discussing it with Bando. What if the profit wasn't all that great and we're basically just selling Nesto's dope.

"Deal, hell yeah." I stated pounding my fist, hoping I wouldn't regret the decision. My gut told me I wouldn't.

"Mijo, I like this little guy!" Nesto yelled rubbing the top of Fernando's head before walking inside his home. Fernando handed me a Corona from the cooler and motioned me to sit in one of the chairs that were scattered around the driveway. I smoothly slid down onto the chair and twisted the top off the beer. I knew damn well I hadn't drunk a beer or any alcohol before in my life. If Donk could see me, now he'll kill Fernando for giving it to me and Nesto, just for being the father of the culprit. Discreetly sniffing the beer before drinking it, the pissy smell made my stomach turn. Although, I was filled with dread, I gulped the beer to calm Fernando's wondering eyes.

"Aaahh." I released. My insides glowed like a pregnant woman's skin and my hands shook in anticipation. I wanted to grip my chest in attempt to subside it, but I didn't want to look weak in front of Fernando. The burning sensation slowly vanished. I sipped from then on. Nesto walked up with a box of Nutty Bars. I was just about to get excited about the chocolate when he threw the box onto my lap.

"I showed you love with that one," he said.

Luckily I didn't speak too soon. He probably would've taken me for a joke.

I decided to call Bando to pick me up instead of Donk. I couldn't chance him questioning me about the box of Nutty Bars. 21 Savage latest mixtape played softly, while I sat at the table watching Bando do his thing and skillfully cut the dope. He retrieved the large blade from the kitchen. The black handle was as long as the blade. However, the blade seemed to be extremely sharp. Using two hands, one on the handle and his other hand on the back of the blade, he swiftly cut the cookie in half while pressing downward, careful to avoid the cookie from crumbling.

"If you don't hit it hard and fast, it'll crumble and you don't want that to happen." He instructed, before repeating the process two more times until the cookie was split into four pieces.

"Aye, what's the tag?" Bando called out.

"Huh?"

"How much you pay for this, boy?"

"$600."

"$600?" Nigga hooked you up for real. This look like a $1500 cookie!"

"I'm going to bust this down in 5s, 10s and 20s, weigh them and bag them up. Me? I don't need a scale, I can eyeball work, but you new to this shit, young blood." Bando continued. I watched on and soaked up all the information possible. Like a student and a tutor, I paid close attention, careful not to break my concentration. It seemed pretty simple. But I know once I get my hands dirty, it'll be a piece of cake.

Bzzzzz! Bzzz!

Arianna: Where are you? When you coming home?

Me: I'm at my patna house. I'll be there in a few.

I quickly responded keeping my eyes on the task at hand.

"Nigga, this $3,000 worth of dope I just bagged up. That's 1500 apiece. You'll profit $900 just sitting there looking pretty. I don't want you to get caught up in this spot. It's easier for me to fend for me alone rather than you. I don't really give a damn 'bout the other nigga that work with me. He grown, but you? Nah, I'm going to hold it down and I'll bring you your cut or you can come pick it up. Long as you breaking bread, I don't mind selling your pack for you.

***

Ring! Ring! Ting!

The ringing of the phone awoke me from my slumber. Me, Arianna and Kadjeah stayed up all night. Cracking jokes, talking shit and watching Netflix and viral videos. Her floor felt good as my bed, due to the fact, Donk purchased expensive carpet to be installed throughout the entire house. The carpet was soft as pillows and it felt even better between my toes.

"Hello." I answered groggily

"Wake up, nigga. Come pick up your shit." Bando was fully alert, like he hadn't been to sleep.

"Wait, you—"

"Aye, we don't do none of that over the phone. Just come see me ASAP! Bando stated before hanging up. I yanked the covers off of me and scurried to my feet, picking up the blanket and pillow dragging it along to my room. Bumping right into Donk, my heartbeat quickened as I looked up into his steely eyes. His gaze was naturally intimidating.

"How you end up with Bando yesterday?"

"Oh, ugghh, Fernando wanted to introduce me to his potna Rosko. This guy has like 100 video games, classic and all the different game systems. We took a break, went outside to shoot hoops and I spotted Bando on the porch talking to a girl so I walked over and asked if he could take me home." I lied.

"Oh, okay" Donk replied rubbing his goatee

"So, where you off to now?" He continued.

"I'm going over Fernando's house." I stated

"Alright cool, get dressed." I had to think of a spot for Bando to meet me with the loot. I couldn't show up to Fernando's empty handed. Nesto might grow suspicious.

***

"Where you going?"

"To a friend of mine house to play video games. What are y'all doing today? I asked pulling my Nike shirt over my head.

"I wanted you to come to the mall with us, but you been gone since the day you got out." Arianna whined.

Bingo! The mall that's perfect. I thought.

"A, I just watched Netflix and shit with y'all all last night, but I'll try and hit the mall if y'all still there. Keep your phone by your side so you can catch my call." I said grabbing my Palm brush off the dresser using my other hand to send Fernando a text.

Me; I'll be over in about an hour.

Fernando: Ok

Me: Pickup from Town East Mall

Bando: Bet

Arianna was still standing in the doorway when I looked up from my phone.

"Yes, Arianna" I surrendered placing my phone and brush inside of my pocket.

186

"You ain't got no swag." She commented crossing her arms over her breast tucking her hands underneath her armpits.

"Okay." I chuckled

"PJ!" Donk yelled.

"Excuse me, I'm bout to go." I stated standing in front of Arianna, who blocked the doorway.

"Can I get by?" I teased a with boyish grin. She rolled her eyes before sliding to the side.

***

"PJ." Donk called turning down the volume.

"Huh?" I responded quickly snapping my head in his direction.

"PJ, I don't want you at that spot." Donk stated with a humorless expression.

"I ain't no preacher, but you already know I don't talk just to be talking." He continued.

"Yes sir." I quickly shot back

"PJ, I'm not playing. If you get caught up over there, it's going to take way more than Steve to get you out. I struggle, sacrifice and take a risk on the daily so my youngins can have whatever. Materialistically speaking, I never once told y'all no. The only time that would part my lips is if y'all asked something that went against my morals." He admitted.

"It's cool if Bando gives you a ride. I don't care if y'all kick it. He fam but there's a difference between a spot and a home. That ain't no home." He continued.

"Yes sir." I needed to take heed to Donks advice but the spirit of greed spoke volumes and I couldn't shake the thought of what was next to come. I didn't want any more handouts. I'm a man and its time I make things happen like one. Donk only made me more focused and dedicated. Watching him and the atmosphere he sets when he's around, the money that seem to ooze from his pores and the undeniable power he possessed I wanted it. I wanted to be like Donk

He unlocked the door and I took that as my cue. I walked into the mall while calling Bando at the same time.

"Yo!" He answered.

"I'm here, where you at?"

"In the parking lot, shooting at this lil' breezy."

"What side are you on?"

"By the Underground Station."

"Here I come." I stated walking back out of the door. I quickly scanned the lot for Donk's truck. When I spotted him merge onto the freeway, I foot it down the sidewalk towards the Underground Station. As soon as I rounded the corner, I spotted Bando leaning on the hood of the car with his head in the window.

"Come on, fam!" I hollered standing by the passenger door of his car. Bando tapped the hood and said something before walking off. Bando was dressed in a Black YSL shirt, black Guess jeans and a pair of black and yellow Kyries.

"What's up fam?" He grinned. "You ready to make this money." He asked enthused. He placed the Styrofoam cup to his lip and took a sip.

"Hell yeah!" I agreed.

"What's the plan?"

"Okay, drop me off and I'll call you to pick me up shortly."

"Bet, here go half." He stated retrieving the money from his pocket and handing it to me before turning the volume up on Lil Uzi's latest mixtape. Bando cradled the cup as if it was a baby. I was curious to know what he was drinking but I didn't have the courage to ask. I sent Fernando a text once we got close.

Me: I'm ten minutes away.

Fernando: Okay me and my pops chilling outside, it was just a brawl across the street. LOL

I smiled, hoping I make it in enough time to see some action. Although, that was my least concern. I sang along to the music, bobbing my head to the beat. We pulled up at Fernando's and I hopped out.

"Just hit me up." Bando called out before pulling off. I walked up the driveway towards Nesto and Fernando. Nesto resembled one of the Mexican dudes on the movie Next Friday, the fat one. He had swag though. He was dripping from his neck to wrists.

"What's up?" I stated dapping both of them up.

"Chiliing, want a beer? He asked reaching into the cooler.

"Nah, I'm good. I would love to sit and chill but I came by to pick up what you promised me. That cookie you sold me was gone by 5 AM this morning. I boasted.

"Oh yeah?" He asked surprised. "You must have sold 50s. How much you make?" He continued.

"Nah, I actually sold 5s, 10s, and 20s and I made three grand." He flashed me Al Pacino's famous mug again.

"Enough said, and for future references never tell a nigga your profit. Your money is your business." He stated before heading inside.

"My pops like you." Fernando said sipping on the beer.

"He say he really sees himself in you. My grandfather is a bit skeptical but that's just him. He should be pulling up any second now." He continued.

"Yeah, he showed love and didn't have to. I feel like he's supportive of my hustle and I respect him for that." I responded. This time Nesto had something bigger than a Nutty Bar box. This time he had a Tide laundry detergent box.

"Aye, it's two bricks in here, homie. I'm about to show you a whole new life. This is just a small investment. I'll make more money having you on the team anyway. I see that hustle and determination in your eyes. I shot Bando a quick text letting him know I was ready.

"Nigga, we got to hurry up and get to our side of the hood with all this in the car." Bando stated paranoid, Shit, he was making me noid.

"Aahhh!" Lil nigga you just don't know how much free money you done put in my pockets! I fuck with you, man." He hollered putting the blunt in his mouth.

"Light that for me." He continued, passing me the blunt. I put fire to the blunt and swiftly passed it back. I didn't want to get into the habit of smoking. Donk always told me drugs were expensive and hard habits to break. Bando freely puffed on the blunt once we came to a stop at the red light.

"Aye, after we break this shit down and come up with a game-plan, you think you can take me back to the mall?" I asked.

"That money burning a hole in your pocket, huh?" He retorted. I chuckled at his statement.

"Nah, fam I told Arianna and Kadejah I would meet them there if everything slowed down. The smile on my face faded and my eyes grew wide in fear. I couldn't warn Bando in enough time before the marked gunman shattered the window with his tool. I could hear my heart beating. Dude had his weapon trained on me as he opened the door to the backseat and grabbed the Tide box.

"Both y'all niggas empty ya' pockets!" The gunman hovering over Bando demanded.

"Fuck you." Bando protested. In one swift motion, the gun-men backhanded Bando in the mouth and the warm liquid gushed down my pants leg onto the floor. I quickly retrieved the money from my pocket and passed it to dude, who had his hand in position ready to strike Bando again

"Here, man! We don't have shit else yo potna just got us for two kilos. That's all we got. Leave him alone!" I babbled. Spooked wasn't the word, I just knew I was going to shit on myself next. The gunmen reached his hand through the window and snatched the $1,500 out my hands before retreating back to his car. Finally able to breathe again, I reclined into the seat as I watched the savage's burn off in the black Mustang.

"You shouldn't have gave that hoe ass nigga shit! If you wasn't in the car, I would've made them niggas work for that shit. Fucking jack boys always trying to take a nigga shit. I'm trapping all day and night for my shit just for a punk to run up on me. Fuck! Where we gone get 70K?"

CHAPTER 24
KADEJAH

"We started off as close friends somehow you turned into my girlfriend. We used to tell each other everything." I sang along to the lyrics of *Close Friends* by Lil Baby and Gunna while I straightened my hair looking into the vanity mirror, Uncle Donk purchased for me on my twelfth birthday. Today was the big day; the day I been waiting all week for. Tru's arrival, I've received a message from her younger sister the other night telling me the good news. I picked out my outfit the day before and laid it over the seat of my chair along with a pair of Jimmy Choo sandals I recently purchased from ALDO's My nerves were so bad I couldn't sleep. I tossed and turned forcing my eyes shut. I managed to doze off a little after 3 AM only to be awaken at 7 AM by Uncle Donk yelling PJ's name. I heavily anticipated this moment since the day I was released.

I'd spoken to Tru once since then. She had someone call me on three way, and I was just enthused it's all over.

"Kadejah, what time we leaving so I can text and tell PJ?" Arianna asked barging in. I jumped at the sudden noise but relaxed when I realized it was just her.

I talked to Uncle Donk. He's swinging by to get us once he post Lil Tim's bond." I responded diverting my attention from my hair.

I'm going to go ahead and get dressed and I'll text PJ once we're done. Ariannawas truly a blessing for the both of us. She was like my shadow. Where I went, she followed and it didn't bother me a bit. Uncle Donk had turned the guest room into Arianna's room and filled her closet with new shoes and clothes. It was happiest I've seen Arianna. I really admired Uncle Donk's generosity. He treated her as his own.

"I loved who you love and mug who you mug." He whispered in my ear when we left the mall that day. I unplugged the pink chi flat irons and ran my fingers through my bone straight hair one last time before getting dressed. I smile to myself as I thought about seeing Lil Tim later after I see Tru. I pulled the YSL crop top over my head, patting my hair down afterwards to ensure every strand was in place. The denim Michel Kors shorts weren't loose but they weren't tight either. Uncle Donk don't play that.

I was starting to become weary but it was absurd for her not to show. What better way to celebrate your first day home?

"PJ doing something he don't have no business doing, so you might as well stop calling him." I commented drinking the Hi-C.

Ring! Ring! Ring!

I quickly grabbed my phone from the bed, as I spotted Uncle Donk's name flash across the screen. "Hello," I answered.

"Hey, come on out so I can drop y'all off. Tim will be released in a hour."

"Let's go! Uncle Donk is out front!" I hollered.

Arianna appeared in the doorway wearing a white Burberry top, creamy cargo shorts, and a pair of red and black Jordan's. "I'm ready," she said.

"You look good but Uncle Donk is gonna make you change those shorts. He'll say they're too tight."

"Well, he bought them a size too small," she said.

"Okay. Come on." I headed out of the house with her behind me.

I noticed the scowl on Donk's face as soon as we climbed in the car. He looked back at Arianna and started fussing about her shorts just as I had warned. She explained that she had failed to try them on before buying them. "I understand, but don't wear them again," he replied.

"Yes, sir." She didn't put up a protest.

I sent a message to Tru's sister letting her know that I was en route. As soon as she responded "Okay" butterflies filled my stomach. My heartbeat quickened in anticipation of embracing her.

***

"What's up?" The two boys appeared out of nowhere. I was so busy daydreaming about Tru, I didn't see them walk up.

192

"Sup?" I responded dryly. They both looked young. One of them had no swag whatsoever, but I couldn't say the same thing about the other one. He looked a bit older too. He sported an orange and navy-blue Polo V-neck, Navy blue cargo shorts, Navy blue and orange bucket hat, with a pair of Navy blue white and dark brown Ralph Lauren loafers. His brown skin was pimple and blemish free and his smile was soothing.

"So, what y'all about to get into?" He asked.

"Were waiting on someone." I responded without making eye contact.

"Excuse me, I'll be right back." Arianna sashayed to the ladies' room. Her butt jiggled with each step. I looked up at the two boys who were gazing at her butt also. They weren't even blinking.

"Say, hey, move around with all of that." I chimed in, breaking their trances.

"Okay, okay. Give her my number!" The one with the swag said, scribbling his number down on the napkin before taking off.

I dialed Tru's sister's number again, but got the voicemail. Once Arianna returned from the restroom, we did a little shopping to pass time, before long hours had passed and I was devastated and ready to go home. I planned to stay longer, thinking I would spend an excessive amount of time with Tru, but that didn't happen. I didn't want to bother Uncle Donk because I'd given him a later time. So, me and Arianna decided to catch a cab. Uncle Donk said Ubers were dangerous. I propped my elbow on the arm of the car door and gazed out the window the entire ride home. I just couldn't understand why Tru didn't show up. She could've at least picked up the phone and told me something, instead of having me waiting around with high hopes. I was crushed I felt like a little girl at her birthday party waiting on her friends from school, but none of them shows up.

Ring! Ring!

I quickly retrieved my phone from my purse, hoping it was Tru. I smacked my lips and reclined on the sofa once I saw Uncle Donk's face.

"Hello?"

"What's up, baby!" Lil Tim yelled into the receiver.

"Heeyyy, Lil Tim, where you at? I grinned jumping to my feet.

"I'm with Donk My phone dead. I'm going to come see you tomorrow. I just wanted to call you and let you know they done let a real nigga out." He stated enthused.

"Okay, I love you. I'LL SEE YOU TOMORROW!"

"Love you, too." I stared at the screen on my phone, seconds after the call ended smiling as I thought about Lil Tim. I wish I was old enough to be in whatever spot he planned on being in tonight. For a minute, I forgot all about Tru standing me up. Arianna walked in the living room. She was dressed comfortable holding a bear in one hand and a bag of chips in the other.

"It's going to be okay, Kadejah," Arianna stated plopping down beside me. We watched SpongeBob reruns as I scrolled through my Facebook news feed. The sun descended and the moon had risen yet I still hadn't heard from Tru. Arianna had fallen asleep, I could hear her snoring lightly from a distance. She looked peaceful and comely. I'm so happy I ran into her that day. Lil Tim had posted multiple pictures of him, Donk and others at a night club. Peering closer at the females it looked as if it may have been a strip club. I clicked on the FB live video as soon as I noticed the notification pop up. Loud music blared from the speaker on my phone, instantly awakening Arianna. I could hear multiple voices. A smile formed across my face when I saw Uncle Donk and some other guy with their arms draped over Lil Tim's shoulder.

"They couldn't hold a real nigga down." Lil Tim slurred loudly. His eyes were so low. If you weren't looking closely, you would think they were closed. He looked so sexy with his fitted cap to the back. His thick eyebrows and luscious lips had me mesmerized. The little time he'd spend in jail, he'd grown a goatee. It wasn't thick, but it was just enough, and trimmed to perfection. You would have thought someone took a ball point pen and drew it on. I tried concealing my lust for Lil Tim from a now awaken Arianna.

"What's that you watching? It's loud." Arianna mumbled rubbing her eyes as she staggered to the couch I was sitting on. Lil Tim turned the camera on different men and women that stood behind him. Chicks were twerking to the music trying to stay close to Lil Tim and his people.

"Fuck with me, you know I got it!" Lil Tim quoted over the loud music. Everyone seemed to be having a blast. One yella' chick in particular stayed glued to Lil Tim's side the whole video and I wasn't feeling that at all. Her face was beat to death and her bundles were curled to perfection. Her tight mesh bodysuit hugged her perfectly. It was a little ho'ish but I give credit when it's due. Arianna hadn't spoken a word. Her eyes were glued to the phone and I could tell she was enthralled by the entertainment.

"I love you, nigga!" This taller, heavier guy shouted drooping his arm over Tim's shoulder.

"I know him." Arianna spoke softly but abruptly as she scanned the house to refresh her memory.

"You don't know him. That's a grown ass man." I added after smacking my lips.

In a mesmerized state she said, "Yes, I do. He was the dude I spotted snooping around the house one day when Persuasia left me home alone."

Ah'Million

CHAPTER 25
LIL TIM

Drunk was an understatement. I didn't know where I was headed but I knew I was safe as I reclined in the backseat of Chris' Magnum, with my hand resting on shorty's thigh. I decided to take this yella bella with me. I didn't even know chick's name. She was so enticing I couldn't pass her up. She promised me a good time and I couldn't turn down the offer. Although, it looked like I was seeing two of her. I made Chris stop by a gas station on the way and pick me up a quart of milk so I could sober up a bit. I was entirely too drunk. I down the milk before he peeled out the gas station

"We here fam. I'm going to grab a change of clothes and head to Keisha's." Chris said stepping out of the Magnum. I didn't give a damn if he stayed or left, I was going to fuck shorty and pass out. The liquor had me feeling awesome and I was fighting to keep my eyes open, yet it was hard when lids felt like they weighed a ton. I staggered out of the whip as I drunkenly draped my arm over shorty's shoulder. She shot me a sexy smile with a little discomfort from practically dragging me. Chris vanished to the back. I flopped down on the plush sofa starting at shortly like she was a piece of steak.

"Come here." I patted the spot beside me.

"Okay, let me get undressed and freshen up." She winked heading down the hallway. I tilted my head back and was about to close my eyes when a framed picture on Chris' shelf caught my eye. Wrinkles formed across my forehead and the left side of my lip curved upward in confusion. I used the arm on the couch to lift myself up so I could get a better view. Once I was to my feet, I slowly walked towards the shelf concentrating on my balance.

"What the fuck?" I mumbled as I noticed Dino's obituary and multiple pictures of him and Chris. Some were just of him and Chris and there were photos with him and a group of women. Some I remember from that night at the Atlanta club. One picture was all too familiar as I looked closely through narrowed slits. It was the bartender chick with the chicks who sucked me. The Sasha or Stasha— whatever her name is chick— and Chris. They were all in cahoots. The feeling of betrayal was evident on my contorted face. I was ready to confront Chris' big ass but I ceased all movement once I felt the cold steel on the back of my skull.

"We better than this, Chris." I didn't want to die young. I didn't want to go out like this. "Chris." I plead spinning around quickly, but to my surprise it was shorty aiming the gun at me.

"Chris dead, nigga, so quit begging!" She spoke in sexy but hurt tone.

"What's the beef? I don't want no smoke." I plead.

"When my brother was begging, you didn't give a fuck. He didn't want no smoke neither. Fuck you!"

CHAPTER 26
DONK

"Why the fuck y'all just now telling me?" I asked angrily. I shot daggers at Bando whose eyes were glued to the floor. If looks could kill, he'll be on a gurney with a white sheet over him.

"I'm sorry, Donk, I was scared I didn't know what to do, but today I got a text from Fernando saying his granddad was sending his workers to my house today at 4 o'clock if I didn't have the money by 3:55," PJ quickly explained. He and Bando stood before me looking pitiful and helpless. Despite the fact that it was dangerous, I had to remain calm and figure something out. Those reckless bets really put a dent in my pocket and 70k wasn't something I wanted to hand over.

"They know where we sleep?" I asked intensely, eyeing PJ.

"Yes, sir. Me and Fernando exchanged addresses in juvie before we parted ways." He admitted.

It was already 3:40 PM and my mind was made, I wasn't coming off no loot. I immediately grabbed my phone from my pocket and called Lil Tim. It rang until his voicemail chimed in so I tried two more times. Nothing. I hadn't heard from Tim in two days since his welcome home party. I sat in the love seat contemplating my next move. If some shit was about to pop off. I had to get Arianna and Kadejah out ASAP but it was just something about PJ's story that didn't sit well with me.

"So, let me get this straight. He gave y'all three days to sell two kilos? I'm saying what made him come down so hard on y'all after three days of having his work?" PJ looked at Bando and Bando looked at PJ as if they were in deep thought.

"Well, Day 2 he wanted to pick up what we made thus far to avoid any careless mishaps, but I was stalling. So, he started blowing up my phone and when I finally picked up, I guess he peeped the bullshit and it went from there." He stated.

"That is a good reason to be skeptical, but it also sounds like y'all were set up, but enough brainstorming. Shit is real. Come on." I stated standing to my feet, removing the robe exposing bare chest and Ralph Lauren pajama pants. I swaggered to the closet inside of my man cave and inserted the code into the keypad. Immediately after entering the code the top half of the wall was replaced with a shelf with rows. On the three rows rested heavy artillery. From Glocks to revolvers, grenades, semi-automatics and shotties. I threw Bando a Mac II and a .45 and told him to throw the Mossberg pump over his shoulder. I stuck a grenade in my pocket. Stuck two Glock .9's in the waist of my pants and grabbed a .223 off the shelf.

"PJ, call Persuasia and tell her y'all on the way," I said, peering at PJ, who was now in tears.

"Why can't I shoot it out with you and Bando?" He asked through sniffles.

"You not shooting shit! You a kid, my nigga! Come on." I led the way. I was so angry I didn't know what to do. Before I could make it up the stairs, Kadejah met me in the front room.

"What's wrong, Unc?" She asked, eyeing my nude chest and massive guns.

"Look, you think you can drive, mama?" I asked dropping to one knee as I gripped both sides of her face with my massive hands.

"Huh?"

"Do you remember everything from that day I showed you how to drive in Skyline's parking lot last year?" I asked trying to refresh her memory.

"Yes, Uncle Donk. I'm sure I remember. Where do you want me to take us?" She looked up at me intensely. The fear in her eyes was evident. I cringed at the thought of PJ's selfishness.

"We not going anywhere." I emphasized pointing at her then me. "You, PJ, and Arianna need to go to Persuasia's, and if she's gone, call her and tell her to come home ASAP. Y'all have to go now! Some real shit is about to pop off and y'all can't be here."

"But, Unc." She attempted to protest.

"Just go, Kadejah!" I yelled kissing her on the forehead releasing my grip. She took out running toward her room constantly looking back. I looked down at my Gucci watch. It was 3:49 PM I ran back down to the study to retrieve my bulletproof vest. As I entered the foyer, Bando had Glocks lined up around his waist tucked inside his Hanes boxer briefs while posing in front of the mirror. "Say man, this ain't no photoshoot!" I yelled shaking my head in disbelief.

"My bad, fam, but I'm ready like Webbie, ya feel me?" He quoted smiling.

Young niggas, I thought, as I quickly retrieved the vest from underneath the bed. I tossed one to Bando and ran to meet up with the kids. "Here, take the Camaro in the garage." I tossed Kadejah the keys. She looked on with shock, when I gave her the keys to my Camaro. She knew the Camaro was my baby. It was the only thing I had left of Mun's. If she didn't know the severity of this madness she did now. "Alright, go now. Get out of here."

PJ was hesitant but I shot him a look you would've thought put fire under his feet, how fast he began to move. I followed them to the garage which led to the alleyway.

"I love you." I mouthed as I pressed the button to raise the garage up. With skill she backed out, whipped the car 'round and sped off. I peered around until the car was out of sight. Pressed the garage door down and sprinted back inside. It was 3:53 PM.

"Fam?" Bando called out standing in the middle of the front room.

"I don't have nothing but love and respect for you, and if I don't make it, make sure my T-lady straight." He stated seriously. Although, I didn't like how Bando handled the whole situation with PJ and Nesto, I couldn't fault him, 'cause when I was PJ's age, I went to the older guys to cop straps so I can go lurking for a come up. I just didn't understand PJ's motive. He had everything a kid could want. I did what I did because I had to. We grew up in poverty. The slam of car doors awakened my survival instincts. I peered out the window and spotted three men and Nesto. Two Hispanic and one black guy.

"You want to split up?" Bando suggested.

"Hell nawl, come on." I swiftly unlocked the windows I had been peering out of and slightly raised it high enough so I could stick my hand out. I fired rapidly at each target. I tried so hard to hit Nesto's fat ass but the 6'2 Hispanic guy jumped in front of him, effortlessly taking the four bullets to the chest before crashing into the cement face first.

Ascending the automatic weapons that rested in their palms, the men fired back rapidly and recklessly. The black guy with Nesto possessed a familiar peculiarity, but with all the chaos and his fitted covering his eyes made it complicated to see his other features. I shrugged it off and stayed focus on keeping my life and protecting Bando's. The automatic weapons tore through the house like Hurricane Katrina. Parts of the padding in the sofa went flying around like pieces of confetti.

"Let's flip this couch over, fam!" Bando yelled crouched down behind the sofa.

"Come on." I stated while flipping the sofa over using it as a barricade to the front entrance. The bullets rang out like these mothafuckas had unlimited ammo. Bullets ripped through the walls chipping the paint and destroying the expensive paintings and IKEA decors. The barrage of rapid fire finally came to a halt, which gave me and Bando time to bust our tools. Sliding from behind the couch and in the entryway of the foyer Bando let the Macc II and .45 spit while I aimed out the already shuttered window. Nesto and his men scattered like ants, but a bullet pierced Nesto in his shoulder causing him to grimace in pain. His fat ass was able to duck on the side of the house before getting his again.

Bando chopped down the wooden fence that was used to surround the garden, and after an extended clip of bullets he was successful.

"Aaarggh!" The Hispanic dude yelped out in pain before collapsing. Bando hit him everywhere, cramming his body with bullets. I could hear Nesto's screams over the gunfire.

Two down, one and half to go. I thought. I chunked the .223 to the side once it stopped clapping.

"You out of ammo, fam?" Bando voiced a little over a whisper.

"Just that piece. I got more artillery. You good?" I asked peering through the window.

"Hell yeah." He stated lifting his shirt, exposing at least three Glocks. "Come on, let's go gun these niggas down. It's really just one left." Bando stated walking towards the front door.

"Nah, let's ju—"

"Get the fuck down." Dude stated. We were so busy looking ahead. We slept on dude's ability. He had come through the back and now we were sitting ducks.

"Donk?" He quizzed once I turned to face him.

"Mun!" I shot back with budging eyes. "I-I thought you were dead." I gasped, then...

Boom! Boom! Boom!

"Noooo!" I yelped as I reached out in attempt to protect Mun, but it was too late. His body dropped. It seemed as if everything slowed down. I looked past Mun and spotted a timid Kadjeah clutching a smoking Glock in both hands.

To Be Continued...
Toe Tagz 3
Coming Soon

Submission Guideline

Submit the first three chapters of your completed manuscript to ldpsubmissions@gmail.com, subject line: Your book's title. The manuscript must be in a .doc file and sent as an attachment. Document should be in Times New Roman, double spaced and in size 12 font. Also, provide your synopsis and full contact information. If sending multiple submissions, they must each be in a separate email.

Have a story but no way to send it electronically? You can still submit to LDP/Ca$h Presents. Send in the first three chapters, written or typed, of your completed manuscript to:

LDP: Submissions Dept
Po Box 870494
Mesquite, Tx 75187

DO NOT send original manuscript. Must be a duplicate.

Provide your synopsis and a cover letter containing your full contact information.

Thanks for considering LDP and Ca$h Presents.

<u>Coming Soon from Lock Down Publications/Ca$h Presents</u>

BOW DOWN TO MY GANGSTA

By **Ca$h**

TORN BETWEEN TWO

By **Coffee**

THE STREETS STAINED MY SOUL **II**

By **Marcellus Allen**

BLOOD OF A BOSS **VI**

SHADOWS OF THE GAME II

By **Askari**

LOYAL TO THE GAME **IV**

By **T.J. & Jelissa**

A DOPEBOY'S PRAYER **II**

By **Eddie "Wolf" Lee**

IF LOVING YOU IS WRONG… **III**

By **Jelissa**

TRUE SAVAGE **VII**

MIDNIGHT CARTEL II

DOPE BOY MAGIC III

By **Chris Green**

BLAST FOR ME **III**

DUFFLE BAG CARTEL **IV**

A SAVAGE DOPEBOY III

By **Ghost**

A HUSTLER'S DECEIT III

KILL ZONE **II**

BAE BELONGS TO ME III

SOUL OF A MONSTER III

Ah'Million

By **Aryanna**
THE COST OF LOYALTY **III**
By **Kweli**
CHAINED TO THE STREETS II
By **J-Blunt**
KING OF NEW YORK V
COKE KINGS IV
BORN HEARTLESS IV
By **T.J. Edwards**
GORILLAZ IN THE BAY V
De'Kari
THE STREETS ARE CALLING II
Duquie Wilson
KINGPIN KILLAZ IV
STREET KINGS III
PAID IN BLOOD III
CARTEL KILLAZ IV
Hood Rich
SINS OF A HUSTLA II
ASAD
TRIGGADALE III
Elijah R. Freeman
KINGZ OF THE GAME V
Playa Ray
SLAUGHTER GANG IV
RUTHLESS HEART III
By Willie Slaughter
THE HEART OF A SAVAGE II
By Jibril Williams

FUK SHYT II

By Blakk Diamond

THE DOPEMAN'S BODYGAURD II

By Tranay Adams

TRAP GOD II

By Troublesome

YAYO III

A SHOOTER'S AMBITION II

By S. Allen

GHOST MOB

Stilloan Robinson

KINGPIN DREAMS II

By Paper Boi Rari

CREAM

By Yolanda Moore

SON OF A DOPE FIEND II

By Renta

FOREVER GANGSTA II

By Adrian Dulan

LOYALTY AIN'T PROMISED

By Keith Williams

THE PRICE YOU PAY FOR LOVE II

By Destiny Skai

THE LIFE OF A HOOD STAR

By Rashia Wilson

TOE TAGZ III

By Ah'Million

CONFESSIONS OF A GANGSTA II

By Nicholas Lock

Ah'Million

PAID IN KARMA II
By **Meesha**
I'M NOTHING WITHOUT HIS LOVE II
By Monet Dragun
CAUGHT UP IN THE LIFE II
By Robert Baptiste
NEW TO THE GAME II
By **Malik D. Rice**
Life of a Savage II
By **Romell Tukes**

<u>Available Now</u>

RESTRAINING ORDER **I & II**
By **CA$H & Coffee**
LOVE KNOWS NO BOUNDARIES **I II & III**
By **Coffee**
RAISED AS A GOON I, II, III & IV
BRED BY THE SLUMS I, II, III
BLAST FOR ME I & II
ROTTEN TO THE CORE I II III
A BRONX TALE I, II, III
DUFFEL BAG CARTEL I II III
HEARTLESS GOON I II III IV
A SAVAGE DOPEBOY I II
HEARTLESS GOON I II III
DRUG LORDS I II III
By **Ghost**

208

LAY IT DOWN **I & II**

LAST OF A DYING BREED

BLOOD STAINS OF A SHOTTA I & II III

By **Jamaica**

LOYAL TO THE GAME

LOYAL TO THE GAME II

LOYAL TO THE GAME III

LIFE OF SIN I, II III

By **TJ & Jelissa**

BLOODY COMMAS I & II

SKI MASK CARTEL I II & III

KING OF NEW YORK I II,III IV

RISE TO POWER I II III

COKE KINGS I II III

BORN HEARTLESS I II III

By **T.J. Edwards**

IF LOVING HIM IS WRONG…I & II

LOVE ME EVEN WHEN IT HURTS I II III

By **Jelissa**

WHEN THE STREETS CLAP BACK I & II III

By **Jibril Williams**

A DISTINGUISHED THUG STOLE MY HEART I II & III

LOVE SHOULDN'T HURT I II III IV

RENEGADE BOYS I II III IV

PAID IN KARMA

By **Meesha**

A GANGSTER'S CODE I &, II III

A GANGSTER'S SYN I II III

THE SAVAGE LIFE I II III

Ah'Million

CHAINED TO THE STREETS
By J-Blunt
PUSH IT TO THE LIMIT
By **Bre' Hayes**
BLOOD OF A BOSS **I, II, III, IV, V**
SHADOWS OF THE GAME
By **Askari**
THE STREETS BLEED MURDER **I, II & III**
THE HEART OF A GANGSTA I II& III
By **Jerry Jackson**
CUM FOR ME
CUM FOR ME 2
CUM FOR ME 3
CUM FOR ME 4
CUM FOR ME 5
An **LDP Erotica Collaboration**
BRIDE OF A HUSTLA **I II & II**
THE FETTI GIRLS **I, II& III**
CORRUPTED BY A GANGSTA I, II III, IV
BLINDED BY HIS LOVE
THE PRICE YOU PAY FOR LOVE
By **Destiny Skai**
WHEN A GOOD GIRL GOES BAD
By **Adrienne**
THE COST OF LOYALTY I II
By Kweli
A GANGSTER'S REVENGE **I II III & IV**
THE BOSS MAN'S DAUGHTERS
THE BOSS MAN'S DAUGHTERS II

210

THE BOSSMAN'S DAUGHTERS III

THE BOSSMAN'S DAUGHTERS IV

THE BOSS MAN'S DAUGHTERS **V**

A SAVAGE LOVE **I & II**

BAE BELONGS TO ME I II

A HUSTLER'S DECEIT I, II, III

WHAT BAD BITCHES DO I, II, III

SOUL OF A MONSTER I II

KILL ZONE

By **Aryanna**

A KINGPIN'S AMBITON

A KINGPIN'S AMBITION **II**

I MURDER FOR THE DOUGH

By **Ambitious**

TRUE SAVAGE

TRUE SAVAGE II

TRUE SAVAGE **III**

TRUE SAVAGE **IV**

TRUE SAVAGE **V**

TRUE SAVAGE **VI**

DOPE BOY MAGIC I, II

MIDNIGHT CARTEL

By **Chris Green**

A DOPEBOY'S PRAYER

By **Eddie "Wolf" Lee**

THE KING CARTEL **I, II & III**

By **Frank Gresham**

THESE NIGGAS AIN'T LOYAL **I, II & III**

By **Nikki Tee**

GANGSTA SHYT **I II &III**

By **CATO**

THE ULTIMATE BETRAYAL

By **Phoenix**

BOSS'N UP **I , II & III**

By **Royal Nicole**

I LOVE YOU TO DEATH

By Destiny J

I RIDE FOR MY HITTA

I STILL RIDE FOR MY HITTA

By **Misty Holt**

LOVE & CHASIN' PAPER

By **Qay Crockett**

TO DIE IN VAIN

SINS OF A HUSTLA

By **ASAD**

BROOKLYN HUSTLAZ

By **Boogsy Morina**

BROOKLYN ON LOCK I & II

By **Sonovia**

GANGSTA CITY

By **Teddy Duke**

A DRUG KING AND HIS DIAMOND I & II III

A DOPEMAN'S RICHES

HER MAN, MINE'S TOO I, II

CASH MONEY HO'S

By Nicole Goosby

TRAPHOUSE KING **I II & III**

KINGPIN KILLAZ I II III

STREET KINGS I II

PAID IN BLOOD **I II**

CARTEL KILLAZ I II III

By **Hood Rich**

LIPSTICK KILLAH **I, II, III**

CRIME OF PASSION I II & III

By **Mimi**

STEADY MOBBN' **I, II, III**

THE STREETS STAINED MY SOUL

By **Marcellus Allen**

WHO SHOT YA **I, II, III**

SON OF A DOPE FIEND

Renta

GORILLAZ IN THE BAY **I II III IV**

DE'KARI

TRIGGADALE I II

Elijah R. Freeman

GOD BLESS THE TRAPPERS I, II, III

THESE SCANDALOUS STREETS I, II, III

FEAR MY GANGSTA I, II, III

THESE STREETS DON'T LOVE NOBODY I, II

BURY ME A G I, II, III, IV, V

A GANGSTA'S EMPIRE I, II, III, IV

THE DOPEMAN'S BODYGAURD

Tranay Adams

THE STREETS ARE CALLING ·

Duquie Wilson

MARRIED TO A BOSS... I II III

By Destiny Skai & Chris Green

Ah'Million

KINGZ OF THE GAME I II III IV
Playa Ray
SLAUGHTER GANG I II III
RUTHLESS HEART I II
By Willie Slaughter
THE HEART OF A SAVAGE
By Jibril Williams
FUK SHYT
By Blakk Diamond
DON'T F#CK WITH MY HEART I II
By Linnea
ADDICTED TO THE DRAMA I II III
By Jamila
YAYO I II
A SHOOTER'S AMBITION
By S. Allen
TRAP GOD
By Troublesome
FOREVER GANGSTA
By Adrian Dulan
TOE TAGZ I II
By Ah'Million
KINGPIN DREAMS
By Paper Boi Rari
CONFESSIONS OF A GANGSTA
By Nicholas Lock
I'M NOTHING WITHOUT HIS LOVE
By Monet Dragun
CAUGHT UP IN THE LIFE

By Robert Baptiste
NEW TO THE GAME
By **Malik D. Rice**
Life of a Savage
By **Romell Tukes**

Ah'Million

BOOKS BY LDP'S CEO, CA$H

TRUST IN NO MAN

TRUST IN NO MAN 2

TRUST IN NO MAN 3

BONDED BY BLOOD

SHORTY GOT A THUG

THUGS CRY

THUGS CRY 2

THUGS CRY 3

TRUST NO BITCH

TRUST NO BITCH 2

TRUST NO BITCH 3

TIL MY CASKET DROPS

RESTRAINING ORDER

RESTRAINING ORDER 2

IN LOVE WITH A CONVICT

Coming Soon

BONDED BY BLOOD 2

BOW DOWN TO MY GANGSTA

Toe Tagz 2

CPSIA information can be obtained
at www.ICGtesting.com
Printed in the USA
LVHW080142290522
719996LV00016B/717